A PISTOL AT MY HEAD

With a girl like Diane Thornton, blonde, beautiful and curvaceous, there were only two options – either you played it smarter than she did or you ran, and kept on running. Jazz pianist Rusty Barlow was too infatuated to run, and didn't realise what he was being pulled into until it was too late. He ran then, and by the time the long arm of the past reached out and grabbed him he was well on the way to success and couldn't afford to get mixed up with a girl like Diane, or a man like Morgan Jackson ... or murder.

A PISTOL AT MY HEAD

by

Anthony Nuttall

Dales Large Print Books
Long Preston, North Yorkshire,
BD23 4ND, England.

British Library Cataloguing in Publication Data.

Nuttall, Anthony
    A pistol at my head.

    A catalogue record of this book is
    available from the British Library

    ISBN   1-84262-294-3 pbk

First published in Great Britain in 1972
by Robert Hale & Company

Copyright © Anthony Nuttall 1972

The moral right of the author has been asserted

Published in Large Print 2004 by arrangement with
Robert Hale Ltd.

Dales Large Print is an imprint of Library Magna Books Ltd.

Printed and bound in Great Britain by
T.J. (International) Ltd., Cornwall, PL28 8RW

Chapter One

I

I had been playing the piano at Meecham's for three months when I met Morgan Jackson again. On my list of the people I least wanted to meet, not only would he have come top but he would have been so far in front of the rest of the field that they wouldn't even count. When I caught the first glimpse of him from the stage I thought that I might be mistaken and it was just someone who looked a lot like him, but when I saw him the second time I knew that there was no possibility of error. Even though I hadn't seen him for over two years there was no mistaking him, tall, broad shouldered and striding about the room as if he owned Meecham's and everyone in it. All I could do now was hope that he wouldn't see me, and a lot of chance there was of that. We play on a stage at one end of the room, and anyone who comes in and wants to know where the music is coming from can't help seeing me.

At the time I'm telling you about, Meecham's was one of the class places for an evening out, though it wasn't too expensive. You could take a girl there, really impress her, and still come out with money in your pockets. I still wasn't sure how I'd finished up there, except that Benny Sugar, who owns the place, happened to like my music and had lured me away from the third rate place I was playing at by offering me a salary which had made my head swim.

He set me up with the rest of the quartet, too. They go under the name of Rusty's Ravers, and there's a big, gold lettered sign above our heads announcing it, but Benny hired them and Benny pays them. Usual stuff. Bass guitar, drums, rhythm guitar, and me on piano. In addition there are two go-go dancers: Pamela, a big-boned, loose limbed, dark-haired girl whom I don't much care for, and Vicki, a compact, well-stacked blonde who learned to dance in Paris and who started at Meecham's just before I did.

We finished one number and there was a sporadic burst of clapping. My hands were trembling slightly on the keys as a result of seeing Morgan Jackson and I was too busy worrying about him to notice much else. I gave an automatic wave to acknowledge the applause and then started on the heavily chorded introduction to our arrangement of In The Still Of The Night. We'd played several fast numbers and this was the one we always used when we wanted to cool things a little.

Pamela and Vicki, one on either side of the stage, went into their slinky routine. A man sitting at one of the tables near the stage gave a faint whistle. Pamela blew him a kiss, and Vicki smiled slightly at him.

Partway through the number the drummer leaned over to me and muttered:

'Ten minutes, Rusty.'

I nodded. We play forty-five minute sets, alternating with a disc jockey called Mad Mike who talks so fast that no one can tell what he says. In spite of that, the birds seem to like him, and a few of his keen fans were starting to move towards the front, ready for when he came on. They ignored me, of course, because the people who like his act don't like mine, but I always take a look at them, just out of interest. Tonight, a waiter pushed his way through them. He handed a note to Vicki who bent down to take it without interrupting her dance, and then placed it on top of the small pile which was already by the piano. They're requests which people send up from time to time; usually we play most of them but tonight there was quite a heap left.

I decided to use one of them to select the closing number. When I picked up the top one and read it my hands began to tremble even more than they had been doing.

'See you after the set, Rusty', it said. There was no signature, just the initials MJ but even without that I would have been able to recognize that square handwriting, and the full stop written as a small circle. I crumpled the note and put it in my pocket, then picked out a request at random.

After the first few bars, I almost lost the tune. I pulled it back and caught Ray, on the drums, grinning at me.

'Who's the bird?' he asked softly, thwacking away at his drums. 'Get your mind off her for the next five minutes and think about the paying customers.'

I laughed and launched into an elaborate improvisation to show that things weren't all that bad. I nearly lost that, too, but it helped to keep my mind off Jackson.

Although Meecham's is such a swank place there's none of this business of a revolving stage. Instead there are two stages side by side and as the curtains slide to conceal me they reveal Mike on the other one with his gear set up and another pair of dancing girls. One of the features of his act is a lot of differently coloured spotlights which he controls himself from a switchboard near the turntable, and as the curtains closed I saw them begin to flash, red, yellow, green, then a steady blue as his voice boomed out.

I sat back on the stool, flexing my fingers.

'Coming for a drink?' the bass guitarist asked me.

'He's got other fish to fry tonight,' Ray said, and winked. 'A bird. That's right, isn't it, Rusty?' A cymbal tinkled as he caught it with his foot.

I stood up.

'I've got other fish,' I agreed, 'but not the kind you're thinking of. Vicki's the only bird for me.'

She turned, her sequinned costume startlingly brief, and I caught my breath. Even after three months of seeing her nearly every night she still had an effect on me that few girls had had, but somehow the idea of a date had become something of a joke between us. That didn't help me, though, and I'd been wondering for a week or two how I could turn things more the way I wanted them to go. She grinned at me now, while Pamela watched us in her dull way.

'I'll see you later,' I said.

'Sure,' Ray answered. 'I'll look after Vicki for you while you're away.'

She squealed as he made a grab for her, and I went through the curtains at the back. From the next stage I could hear the booming and twanging of the pop music, but for once it didn't irritate me as much as usual. In the circumstances in which I'd come to London from the North, any meeting with Morgan Jackson was going to be a bad one, and I was too bothered with him to worry about anything else.

I made my way along the dusty passage at the back of the stage, passed the couple of rooms which the girls use as dressing rooms, and through a yellow door which leads into the main part of the club. I couldn't see Jackson in the gloom but I guessed he would be watching for me. I wasn't wrong. After I'd stood by the door for a couple of minutes, watching Mike, who looked like a devil with the full glare of a red lamp on him, Jackson popped out of the crush and came towards me.

He hadn't changed a bit. Well made, powerful looking, walking with a solid tread as if he was going to let no one get in his way. Generally, he wouldn't. People who got in Morgan Jackson's way were trampled underfoot, like I'd been, and left to sort their own way out of it.

He worked his cigar to the other side of his mouth and looked at his watch.

'How long have you got, Rusty?'

'Half an hour.'

'That should be long enough. Coming for a drink? Or aren't you allowed to while you're on duty?'

'I'm allowed to,' I answered calmly, refusing to be needled by his sneering attempt to put me at a disadvantage.

'Then what are we waiting for?'

He turned, pushing his way past everyone, and I followed him to the bar. He stood by, smiling faintly, while I signed a chit for the drinks. It would have been all the same if I'd had to pay for them. We carried them to a table at the far side of the room; a couple of acquaintances smiled at me and I managed a smile back. I still didn't know what Jackson wanted, and until I did I was going to be very edgy and very wary.

He didn't seem in any hurry to tell me.

'Come up in the world since I saw you last,' he said, gulping his beer like a pig at the swill. 'How come you're playing piano at a joint like this? You were just a punk electrician when I knew you.'

'I've taken my chances as they've come,' I said, sipping my own drink. 'Why should you worry what happens to me, anyway? And what are you doing here tonight?'

'I've come to enjoy myself. Is it profitable, playing the piano?'

'What's it to you?'

'Listen, Barlow,' he said, a flash of anger showing through because I wasn't meekly answering his questions, 'I do all the asking here. Right? It doesn't matter to me how much you get from Meecham's but it might matter to you. Now answer the question. Is it profitable?'

'I don't go short,' I said mildly.

'I've a job for you.'

'I don't want one,' I told him calmly, though I was starting to sweat. 'I'm happy here.'

He gulped some more beer. I drank mine more slowly, waiting for the next move. One thing was certain. I didn't want to work for Jackson but if he'd made up his mind that I was going to, I wouldn't have much chance; he knew too much about me for me to risk arguing with him too much.

He set his glass down heavily.

'I said I'd got a job for you, Rusty, boy,' he said. 'You've got special talents and I want to use them. I'm not asking you to work for nothing, don't think that. Is that what's worrying you?'

'You're worrying me,' I said, 'but I suppose I'll have to listen whether I want to or not.'

'It'll only take you a week or so, and whatever they pay you here for a month, I'll double.'

'Two months' salary for a week's work?' I asked, my eyes narrowing. 'You must want me pretty bad. Isn't there anyone else you can use?'

'You know how it is.'

'I know how it is. You'll want to be certain that I'll keep my mouth shut afterwards and you don't know anyone else you can put that kind of pressure on. That's the only reason you want to use me, not because I've got something special.'

'You've got something special, Rusty, boy,' he insisted. 'I'm going to use you so you might as well make your mind up to it.'

That's just how he always was. Arrogantly assuming that everyone would do just what he wanted. It took a lot of effort, but I

13

laughed at him.

'What sort of a job is it? What do you want to knock off?'

He smiled, showing his snowy-white slab teeth which were massive and purposeful, like everything else about him.

'I'm offering you a job,' he repeated. 'Are you going to take it or do I have to persuade you?'

'I don't want anything to do with it,' I said bluntly. 'I work here. I'm on the way up and that's the way I'm going. Working for you would kill everything that I've built up these last two years. I don't know what your job is but if it's like the rest of you it'll be something rotten and filthy that I wouldn't want to touch if I had to beg for bread in the streets.'

I started to push my chair back and get up but he put his hand on my arm, his eyes glittering.

'Don't go yet, Rusty,' he said, his voice quiet. 'Rotten and filthy I might be but I've never killed a man. There are maybe one or two things that you don't understand about what I'm saying to you.'

I sat down again. I'd been expecting him to take this line, with what he knew about me, and I was ready for him.

'You can't prove a thing,' I said. 'You can

talk, but try and prove it.'

'I don't have to prove anything. All I have to do is slip the word to the cops and they'll easily do all the proving, even after two years. When they reckon they've got enough they'll come and see you, and where are you then? If you've any sense you'll have got the hell out of it. Whatever else happens you won't be on the way up any more, and all because you wouldn't do a job for me. For old time's sake.'

'Old time's sake!' I exclaimed. 'How long have you been planning this, Morgan? Who told you I was here? I haven't seen or heard of you for two years and now you turn up like this.'

'And it's given you a shock. I can't help that, Rusty.'

'Who told you I was here?'

'No one,' he said mildly. 'I've left the North now, you know, and come to live down here, like you. It was pure chance that I happened to see you thumping that piano but when I got to thinking about it I realized that you were ideal for what I've got in mind.'

'I don't want your filthy job!'

'You're going to have it, whether you want it or not, so you might as well get used to the idea. Don't forget that I can give the cops all the information they'll need.'

'And when they come for me what do you think I'll tell them about you?'

'You won't tell them a damned thing,' he said, his voice soft in the crowded bar. 'You don't even know where to find me. You can't give them my address or say anything at all about me. And if you do, there's only your word and not a thing anyone can prove.' His voice changed to a sneer. 'And who's going to take the word of a killer?'

I swallowed.

'You know as well as I do that it was an accident,' I said, without much hope.

'The cops won't see it that way. All things considered, to them it's murder.'

I put my glass down on the table and began to poke it round in a small circle with the tip of my finger. Out of the corner of my eye I saw the door open and Ray and Vicki come in. The brief crash of pop music was cut off as the door swung shut. Vicki was wearing a green dress instead of her stage costume. She smiled and Ray waved as they spotted us; they started towards our table, then Ray saw that Jackson was with me and changed his mind.

'Friends of yours? Jackson asked.

'He plays the drums behind me.'

'And isn't that bird one of the dancers?' He winked and leered at me. 'I could use an hour with her any time she likes, Rusty, boy.'

'Let's leave Vicki out of it,' I said, feeling my face getting hot but not being able to do anything about it.

'Like that, is it?' He leaned back and looked at me thoughtfully. 'I'd watch it if I were you, Rusty. You could easily make a fool of yourself over a girl like that.'

'Suppose I did take this job,' I said slowly, wanting to get his mind off Vicki, 'what would I do?'

'Can't discuss details here, boy,' he said. 'You ought to realize that.'

'I do but I just wanted to make sure.' I poked the glass some more. 'So where would I discuss the details?'

'I'll give you an address,' he replied, 'and if you go round there tomorrow night we can get everything sorted out.'

'I take it it's something criminal?'

He didn't say anything to that, which was as good an answer in itself as anything he could have said.

'I'm not working tomorrow night,' I said slowly.

'I've already checked that out.'

I flushed.

17

'Do you have to be so smart?'

'In my line of business, yes. The ones who are not so smart get in trouble. Do you want this address?'

'Have I a choice?' I asked bitterly.

'If you go out to Chelsea and you find the King's Road and go along it until you come to a street called Turpin Street, then drive along there for a couple of minutes you'll come to Wagstaffe Place. It's a block of flats. I don't live there but I've rented one under a false name. On the first floor, flat five. You come there at eight o'clock tomorrow night and we'll sort out all the details.'

'Will anyone else be there?'

'Could be. You won't be in this on your own, Rusty, don't worry about that.'

'Meaning that you've lined up a few of us to carry the can if anything goes wrong? And what will you be doing? Nothing if my guess is right.'

He laughed.

'I'm on the way up, like you. I stopped taking risks a long time ago. That's why I'm still around.' He glanced at his watch. 'You've only got five minutes of your half hour left. Hadn't you better be getting back?'

'Perhaps I'd better.' I stood up and went towards the door. I couldn't see Ray and

Vicki anywhere, which meant that they must have got a couple of bottles and taken them back to the stand. If I hurried there might be some left when I got there, and I reckoned I needed a quick drink without Jackson to be in good enough shape for the next set.

'Don't forget,' he said as he followed me out of the bar. 'Eight o'clock tomorrow night.'

When I turned round to answer him he'd already gone, swallowed up in the crowd, and that made my neck tingle for a start; if he didn't really want to be seen with me it was going to be a bad job.

Whatever kind of job it was, I was going to have to do it, unless I thought fast.

II

To explain the hold that Morgan Jackson has over me, and why I was so afraid of him, I'm going to have to go back about two years, to a time when Meecham's hadn't been thought of and was still a block of cramped offices, and to time when the only piano playing I did was at parties. I was living in Manchester then, working as what Jackson had called a punk electrician, and didn't even meet him until about six months after the events which led up to all this had started.

It was someone who worked with me at a firm called Strong's, who made and fitted burglar alarms, who invited me to the party where I met Diane Thornton. When the time came, he was ill and couldn't go and as most of the other guests were friends of his whom I didn't know I was at something of a loose end. I mooched around the big house for a while, trying to talk to various people who were in cliques of their own, and then found myself in an empty room, with a piano.

One of the things I've always been able to do is play the piano, and when I was a kid I had ideas of becoming a concert pianist. I actually learned one or two of the simpler pieces, but then the constant slog of practising, and the near certainty of never actually earning big money at it, put me off, and after hearing a Count Basie record at a friend's I turned to jazz.

There was still little chance of making money at it, but I reckoned that as jazz music probably appealed to more people than the classical stuff, the odds were slightly better. Anyhow, I settled down in any spare moments with my pile of George Shearing,

Basie, Fats Waller and Earl Hines records on one side of the stool and a heap of sheet music on the other, and worked away at it.

It didn't take long to discover that my talents were more for imitation rather than evolving a new style but once I accepted that I didn't come along too badly. I was nowhere near good enough to earn money at it, of course, so when I left school the relations with whom I was living pushed me into the apprentice electrician job at Strong's.

As soon as I could, I got a flat of my own. All my life I'd been shunted around from aunt to aunt, and that was one thing I'd always promised myself as soon as I started work. Three months after starting with Strong's I was in a flat with a piano which I'd bought for a fiver from someone who was going to Australia. It wasn't long before I had a new circle of friends, and I found that because I could play the piano I was invited to quite a lot of parties.

It was one of these, as I've said, that I met Diane Thornton.

As soon as I saw that piano in the empty room I couldn't resist the urge to sit down at it. The main worry with a strange piano is that some of the notes may be broken, but as soon as I'd checked they weren't I took the soft pedal off and began to pound it out. When Diane came in I was running through a boogie version of Basie's Feather Merchant which I'd lashed up myself from various recorded versions. I wasn't too happy with parts of it and when I saw the door open and a pert blonde wearing one of the shortest skirts I've ever seen, before or since, come in, it threw me completely. I finished abruptly in a clatter of discords and started to shut the lid.

'Don't let me stop you,' she said with a smile, putting a half full glass of something on top of the piano. 'Would you mind if I stayed here and listened to you?'

I opened the lid again and ran my hands lightly over the keys.

'I wouldn't mind in the least,' I said swallowing, 'but I'd rather you sat where I couldn't see you. Not that I mind looking at you,' I added hastily, 'but–' I broke off in some confusion, and played a few chords to cover up my embarrassment.

'I know exactly what you mean,' she said, smoothing down her skirt so that there could be no misunderstanding. 'Just forget that I'm here.' Taking her drink she sat down in an armchair behind me, and crossed her legs.

I turned back to piano. After a moment's thought I pulled out of my memory a couple of boogies which I've played for several years and which I think I could manage in my sleep. I went straight from one to the other and then into a slow version of Honeysuckle Rose which I'd taken off an ancient Fats Waller record.

After about ten minutes I looked round at her.

'How come there's nobody else in here?' I asked. 'I don't play that badly, do I?'

She shook her head. Her shoulder length hair tumbled about with the movement and I watched, fascinated.

'No one will disturb us,' she said, finishing her drink. 'They've persuaded Jackie Dawson to do a striptease in the other room but I'm not interested in watching another girl take off her clothes. If she wants to do it, that's her affair, but I'd rather be with the men.' She laughed as she said that, a warm, throaty sound that made emotions crawl up and down my back. 'Unless you'd like to go and watch, that is?'

'No,' I said. 'No, I'll stay in here.'

I should have gone. If nothing else the entertainment in the other room was free; the entertainment I got from Diane Thornton was the most expensive I've ever had.

She set it up very nicely. I was a kid then, about twenty, and she'd be perhaps twenty-five. It never occurred to me to wonder what she was doing going around with someone like me; it never crossed my mind that her league was with the swingers, the club owners, the big money operators, and to wonder what she was doing with an electrician who did nothing more exciting than wire up burglar alarms.

I realize now that she'd been working with Morgan Jackson all along. They'd warned us at the factory that smart characters might pressure us for details of the circuits we installed, and in fact before we could work on certain jobs we had to have a clearance check, just to make certain we weren't going around with the wrong people. At the start I'd had some idea that this might be what Diane was after, but as the months passed and she made no mention of it, it dropped further and further from my mind. I carried on making a fool of myself with her, although I didn't think of it like that at the time, and I woke one morning to the realization that not only did I have hardly any money but I owed nearly three hundred quid to a bloke whose name I'd got from Diane.

I didn't worry too much about it until a knock came at the door the next night.

'I think you've come to the wrong place,' I said when I went to answer it. He was a big, hulking bloke wearing a shabby raincoat and with a face that looked as if they'd lost the pattern when they'd come to him and had to try and make it from memory.

He pushed his thick lips into something that might have been meant as a smile.

'You Rusty Barlow? he asked.

I nodded.

'Then I haven't come to the wrong place,' he said. 'I just want to remind you that you owe Mike Deany three hundred quid. Haven't forgotten it, have you?'

'I haven't forgotten it.'

'And what are you going to do about it?' He was standing on the small landing outside the door; as he spoke he wedged his foot in the door and gave me another of those smiles.

'I'll pay it back soon,' I said, as clearly as my dry mouth would permit. 'Tell Deany to quit worrying.'

'He'll quit worrying when he gets his money,' he replied. 'As soon as you like.'

Without any apparent effort he gripped the edge of the door in his massive hands, one at the top and one about halfway down, just below the handle. He gave a twist and there was a snap and tearing of wood as the hinges were wrenched away from the post. The bottom of the door hit the carpet with a dull thud. He dusted his hands together.

'Wouldn't like to have to do anything like that to you,' he said, and walked away.

Because I didn't want to make a bad impression on Diane I didn't say anything to her, even though she knew Deany, but I worried plenty. The trouble didn't stop there, either. Other people came to see me. None of them twisted the door off its hinges but one of them loosened two of my front teeth with his head and another one made a little heap of crumpled newspapers in the middle of the carpet one night while I was out, and set fire to them. Not much damage was done but a phone call the day after suggested that I'd be wiser not to leave things too long.

It dawned on me that I had to have money, and I had to get it fast.

And all the time my wages were being sucked away by Diane. She'd had me buy an old car, which was eating holes in my pocket, we went drinking and clubbing a lot of nights, and I felt that unless I put on a show I'd risk losing her.

And I didn't want to lose her. Not then, at any rate.

It was on one of the club trips that we met Morgan Jackson. He didn't appear to be a friend of Diane's, and he introduced himself to us by stumbling as he passed our table and spilling half a glass of beer down the front of her dress. He was more charming then than I've ever seen him since, getting waiters to run around with cloths, giving us his address, telling us to send the cleaning bill on to him, and so on.

At Diane's suggestion I took the bill round to him myself. It wasn't as much as I'd expected, but he gave me a fiver and waved away the change as he offered me a drink.

'Don't worry about that, boy,' he said. 'Keep it for your trouble. Buy her something with it, soothe her feelings a bit.' He winked at me, and told me to sit down.

Anyone who could wave money around as freely as that interested me, and we sat and talked about this and that for a few minutes. Eventually he asked me where I lived, and raised his eyebrows when I told him I was an electrician at Strong's, the burglar alarm people.

'Come across some interesting stuff in

that line of business, won't you?

'Sometimes. Not often.'

I didn't want to talk about it too much. We'd just finished a big job and I was still security conscious. I sat back and looked around the flat, comparing it with my own dump and wondering how I could afford a place like this. Antique furniture which looked expensive, though I didn't care much for it. The biggest television set I've ever seen. Thick carpet.

Jackson was clever, and though he must have noticed my interest he didn't try to press me then, nor did he mention the burglar alarms again that day except to say that there could be big money in some of the circuit details.

I heard from him again a week later, after the idea had had chance to sink into my head. This time he was more like the Morgan Jackson I was to come to know, telling me that he knew all about my money troubles and that he had a good way to solve them for good. I was a bit abrupt with him on the phone, but I agreed to meet him.

He got straight to the point.

'You've been doing some work on Fingal's warehouse, haven't you, putting in a new alarm?'

'How do you know that?' This was just after I'd had another visit from a couple of thugs pressing for payment, and my arm was very stiff after what they'd done. I flexed it slowly and looked at him.

'I find things out, Rusty,' he said. 'It doesn't matter how it's done as long as it's right. Is it?

'Yes,' I said, after a moment's hesitation.

'Feel like making a couple of thousand quid?'

I swallowed. A couple of thousand was just what I needed. With that I could solve all my problems with Deany and have a fair bit over to spend.

'How would I do that?' I asked, still wary in spite of myself.

He smiled.

'I've got to trust you, Rusty,' he said. 'I'm going to put something to you now and you could go straight out of here and run to the cops and tell them everything. If you should feel like that, remember that Mike Deany is a friend of mine and that you owe him three hundred quid. If I told him you were plan-ning to skip town he'd get real mean, don't you think?'

'Probably he would.'

'In fact,' he went on, looking at me over

the rim of his glass, 'I could tell him that anyway. See what I mean, Rusty?'

I saw what he was getting at all right. Either help him or be finally and thoroughly worked over by the thugs he was in with. Too late I realized the trap I'd been pulled into. Even at that stage I couldn't think that Diane had had anything to do with it, though when I went over everything a long time afterwards I saw how she'd managed things from the start.

'Well?' I said to Jackson. 'What do you want me to do?'

'I'm thinking of pulling a little job,' he said softly. 'I happen to know that there'll be fifteen thousand pounds worth of furs in Fingal's warehouse next weekend. Never mind how I know. I want to get them out of there but I don't know enough about the alarm set up to be sure of getting in the place safely.'

I didn't speak. He tossed back the rest of his drink and put his glass down on the table in front of us.

'They tell me there's something special about Fingal's alarm,' he went on. 'You put it in and you should know if there is anything funny.'

'I was only one of the blokes who put it in,'

I told him, making a weak attempt to get out of it.

'What did you say Mike Deany's number was?'

'All right, all right,' I said hastily, 'I know about Fingal's alarm and I know the little tricks it plays if you don't treat it right. I also know how to stop it.'

He dropped the receiver back onto its prong.

'That's better, boy. I think we should have a little talk. Tell me about this alarm.'

'It's just a normal system on the face of it,' I said. 'Once it's switched on, opening any doors or windows on the outside of the building sets off a recording in the local police station. They come round and get you while you're still climbing in.'

'I know all about things like that,' he said impatiently. 'What's the other part?'

'The other part is that there's a secondary system which works on the internal doors. In other words you can put the outside one out of action and get in but as soon as you open any doors inside the building you still set the alarm off. There are other things like pressure pads in the floor and light beams across some of the doors, too.'

He grunted.

31

'So how do we get round all that?'

'The best way of getting round the pressure pads and the light beams is to avoid them,' I said, 'but to do that you have to know where they are. I can give you that. The internal wiring you deal with in just the same way as the one outside. There's nothing hard about it, but most people wouldn't know that the two systems are there and that's where they'd come unstuck. Provided you can bridge the doorways so that there's no break in the circuit when they're opened, you're all right. You can work your way down to the main fuse boxes and deactivate the whole system. Once you've managed that you can do what you like.'

'And you can fix all this?'

'I can fix it if it's worth my while. What's my cut out of this fifteen thousand pounds?'

He laughed.

'You're in no position to bargain, Rusty. I've told you what your share is. You get enough to take Mike Deany and his boys off your back and leave you some over for kicks. And you can carry on with that classy blonde you've got lined up.'

I flushed at that, trying to think of something to say that would take the sneer out of his voice and show him that he hadn't completely got the upper hand. Before I could open my mouth he was off again.

'Is there a watchman at Fingal's, do you know?'

'There wasn't when I did the job. That was only about six weeks ago so things shouldn't have changed much.'

'That'll do me. I'll lay on a van that the cops won't be able to trace back to us and we're in business. We'll go round there, and–'

'Just a minute,' I broke in, 'I never agreed to that. I'll tell you exactly what to do with the alarm and I'll draw you a plan of the pressure pads and so on, but I'm not going round there myself. If you think I'm getting mixed up in that kind of racket, you're wrong.'

'You're the one who's wrong, Rusty, boy,' he said. 'You're already mixed up in it.'

'I'm not doing it myself,' I insisted.

'You'll do it yourself and like it, boy. Either that or I'll get Deany's boys to break your neck and cut that bird of yours up so that men will run screaming when they see her.'

There was a tense silence. I didn't mind the threat to myself so much but I didn't feel that I could let Diane in for that kind of trouble. I argued with him some more but it was hopeless and no one knew it more than me. He had too much leverage and too much skill in applying it, and in the end I had to agree. I had no more chance of beating him than I had of finding the money to pay Mike Deany without getting drawn into something criminal.

'I think Saturday night will be the best time to do it,' he said after I'd lost the argument. 'Are there any tools that you'll need?'

'I can get them from work without any trouble.' I paused. 'It might only seem a small point to you but Strong's will think there's something funny when they hear about it. So will the cops. Seeing as I put the alarm in, won't they come to have a word with me?'

'They might. You're not George Washington are you?'

'Huh?'

'You don't have to tell them the truth. If you say you don't know anything about it they won't have a leg to stand on. In any case, why should they think of you? There've been break-ins at places you've wired up before, haven't there?'

I nodded.

'And did the cops come to see you then?'

'No, but–'

'But it wouldn't have mattered if they had

because you weren't involved. I'll tell you what. Just to make sure, you'd better give me a list of those tools and I'll get them for you. I don't want some stupid slip up over someone seeing you taking a load of tools home on the Friday night.'

There were no stupid slip ups over the tools, thanks to Jackson. There was only one slip up, but that was enough, and it was partly my fault for not getting him to check some of the information that I'd given him.

During the week I thought about what he'd said and what I could do about it. As far as I could see, if I repaid the money I owed to Deany then Jackson would have no hold over me; the only trouble was that I had no hopes of repaying anything, and definitely not before the weekend. The only idea I had was that I could appeal to Deany directly, but that wouldn't do much good. Someone who uses thugs like that as debt collectors isn't going to let words influence him very much. In any case, he was probably in for a cut of the fifteen grand and it was in his interests not to take the money.

I was hooked.

If my bosses at Strong's noticed anything strange about my attitude during that few days they didn't say anything and neither did anyone else. I worked as normally as I could, and spent the evenings sitting in, watching the television, shuddering at the efficiency of the cops I saw on it and trying to convince myself that they weren't like that in real life. Diane had told me that she had to go away on business for a few days; I accepted that at the time but I can see now that it was all part of the plan.

It was cold and trying to rain on the Saturday night. I met Jackson at a pokey little pub in the city centre, squashed between two large office blocks, and after a quick drink we drove out to Fingal's warehouse. Jackson had nicked the van and got false number plates; I drove. When we drew near the warehouse I stopped in a side street and switched off the engine.

'Well?' I asked. My nerves were taut. The streets were pitch dark, lit only by a pair of flickering gas lamps which the council hadn't got round to replacing.

'Just a few last minute arrangements, boy,' Jackson said easily, opening the window to throw away his cigarette end. The cold night air blew in and I shivered. He closed the window then leaned into the back, hefting a bag over and dropping it between us. 'These all the tools you'll want?'

I checked them quickly. Everything I'd asked for was there, and I nodded. They weren't new but I didn't bother asking where he'd got them. He pushed something into my hand.

'You might need this, too, if there's any lumber.'

I stared at the gun he'd given me.

'Now wait a minute–'

'I hope you don't need it,' he said, 'but there might be lumber. You never know. If there is you can use it to frighten people. It works wonders.'

'I've never used one before.'

'Nothing to it.' He pointed. 'Slide that back. Now when you pull the trigger it'll fire.'

If I'd had any sense I'd have shot him there and then and cleared off, but I didn't. My mouth was too dry to speak so I merely nodded at him, then laid the gun on my knee, with the safety catch back on, while I took out the thin cotton gloves he'd told me to bring. After putting them on I wiped the gun carefully and gave him a sarcastic smile.

'Is that right?'

'Let's get on with it,' he said. 'Never mind the funnies. Time enough for them when it's over.'

We got on with it. There were no problems. I drove the van round to an alley nearer the warehouse and while Jackson held the torch I killed the alarm and opened the window. We climbed in. He took a rag from his pocket and covered the torch glass with it, using an elastic band to hold it in place. The muted glow that everything was bathed in made it seem even more eerie, and I shivered.

'This way,' he whispered.

We crept about. He seemed to know the layout as well as I did and he also knew exactly where the furs were. We worked out a route from them to the van which would use the least number of doors and I bypassed the alarm circuit on each one. When the police did start looking into it there would be less suspicion against me than there might be if I'd shown that I was too familiar with the wiring of the fuse box.

That only left the problem of the pressure pads, which could still trigger the system if either of us trod on one. I showed Jackson where they were fitted, and the only safeguard was to go carefully and let me lead the way once we knew the route.

'That's the tricky one,' I said showing him one that stretched right across the passage. 'For God's sake watch it when you come up those steps. If you fall, we've had it.'

'I'll go easy. I've done this sort of thing before.'

It was very silent in the huge building. The only noise was the padding of our feet as we shuffled back and forth with the armfuls of furs, pausing before we actually got to the van to make sure that no coppers had turned up since the last trip.

'We should have had a lookout,' Jackson said after the first trip, 'but it's hard to get anyone reliable these days. In any case you've got to start giving too many people a cut if you aren't careful.'

I said nothing. All I wanted to do was to get the job over with and clear off. My troubles would start on Monday, when Strong's heard about it. I'd tucked the gun into the top of my jeans, and I was very conscious of it banging against me as I walked.

It was on the last trip that trouble cropped up.

There was only one armful of furs left. I was carrying it while Jackson walked in front of me with the torch. When we were nearly at the exit we'd made for ourselves there was a sudden noise behind me, a kind of light footfall, and a light flashed on. At the same moment a voice shouted:

'I told you I heard a noise!'

I heard Jackson exclaim as I blinked in the sudden light, almost blinded by it. By the time I could see again Jackson was near the window and another voice was shouting.

Dropping the furs, I ran. I collided with someone and there was a confused scuffle with a wiry bloke while another man shouted: 'Get the swine. Kick his face in!' Wrenching myself free I ran towards the window, where Jackson was already halfway out.

Footsteps pattered behind me. I reached the window and turned, dragging out the gun. If I could startle the bloke and frighten him for only a couple of seconds it would give us more chance of reaching the van and getting away.

I looked straight into the eyes of one of the maintenance men I'd worked with when I'd been installing the alarm. His name was Dave Stewart, and from his expression I knew that he'd recognized me.

In a flat panic, hardly realizing what I was doing, I pulled the trigger. The gun recoiled more than I'd expected and jarred my arm right up to my shoulder. Stewart had been jumping towards me. The slug caught him in the chest, stopping him suddenly and definitely. He hung in the air for a second or two then just crumpled up and hit the floor with a soggy sound like a couple of hundred-weights of dough falling down a chute.

His mate, the wiry bloke I'd been fighting with, was keeping well back. I don't think he even noticed me, he was so horrified by what had happened to Dave Stewart.

I scrambled out of the window, trembling so much that I didn't know what I was doing. Had Jackson not waited for me and grabbed my arm to pull me through I don't think I'd have made it; as it was we got back to the van just as the bloke who'd been with Stewart started yelling out of the window. Jackson slid into the driving seat. I'd left it in gear and he started the engine and drove off in one smooth movement.

I slumped in the passenger seat, the gun still in my hand. After a few seconds I reached up mechanically, slid the window back and tried to stuff the gun out into the road, concerned only that it shouldn't be found anywhere near me. Jackson saw what I was doing. He grabbed my arm and leaned across me to shut the window again. The van swerved wildly and a car coming the other way flashed its headlights.

'Leave it,' Jackson said, wrenching the van

back on its own side of the road. 'I'll get rid of it.'

'Did you see what happened?' I asked. My teeth were chattering and I could hardly get the words out.

'You killed him,' he said. 'You know that? I saw it all.'

I nodded. Even when I closed my eyes I could see Stewart's face and the expression that had been on it when he had recognized me. It had changed when the slug had hit him, and that too was something I'd never forget.

'He knew who I was,' I said. 'Fingal's told him to help us with the alarm so that he'd know the layout.'

'He knows the layout now all right,' Jackson said, whistling through his teeth. 'Armed robbery. You're in bad, Rusty, boy. Better let me handle this.'

'I'll handle it,' I said roughly. I might have been dazed by what I'd just done but I wasn't so far gone that I was going to get in any deeper with Morgan Jackson.

'You don't know what you're doing.'

'I'll think about it. Drop me off at my place and I'll see you in the morning.'

'If you're still in that state on Monday you'd better phone Strong's and tell them you're not so well. If they see you like that you won't stand a chance. Did that other guy see you?'

'I don't think so.'

'That's something to be glad of.'

I nodded. As the full extent of what I'd done began to get through to my mind I could feel myself sinking into a kind of stupor. Jackson didn't say anything else and I slumped in my seat for the rest of the journey, watching the lightly falling rain spatter the windscreen. I was dimly aware that we had reached my flat. I got out of the van, told Jackson that I'd see him in the morning and stumbled up the stairs without waiting for an answer. I didn't meet anyone, and I was glad.

It took me a long time to get to sleep. When I finally managed it I seemed to see Stewart's face all night. He was looking at me reproachfully and although his lips were moving no sound was coming out and I couldn't tell what he was saying.

I woke early the following morning and lay in bed, listening to the Sunday silence. Last night's events were still vivid and terrible in my mind but the vision of the dead man's face had faded slightly. The little bit of sleep had had the effect of clearing my mind and though I was still tired and dopey I could see a lot of things for what they were.

To any crook like Jackson someone with a good knowledge of alarm systems would be a boon. Through Diane he'd cultivated me and the further into debt she got me, the better it had suited his plans. When he'd considered that I was ripe, he'd jumped. Probably he intended to drag me in even further now. Borrowed money was one thing but murder was a new hold, something he'd be able to use to get me to do almost anything he wanted.

But there was no proof.

He wouldn't need any proof. The cops would dig that our fast enough once they'd had the tip off.

There were two things I could do. Either get rid of Jackson, or clear out.

The thought of killing someone else made me feel sick, and I chose to clear out. About half an hour after I'd made the decision Jackson came knocking at the door, but I didn't let him in. I sat in the kitchen while he pounded on the front door. Faintly I could hear him calling something, but I stayed where I was until the sounds ceased and I heard a car driving off.

My plans were simple. By mid-afternoon

I'd loaded everything that belonged to me into my car, written a letter to the landlord to say that I was giving up my flat, and enclosing the rent which was owing, and written to my boss at Strong's to say that I'd been called urgently to my sister in Glasgow and I didn't know how long I'd be away.

Not that I'd any intention of going to Glasgow. I was headed in the opposite direction, two hundred miles down the M1, to London. I didn't know anyone there and I'd no idea why I chose it except that it seemed to me a place that it would be easy to hide in, easy to forget the past and easy to start all over again.

By nine o'clock that evening I was halfway down the motorway with fifty-seven pounds in my pocket, which was all the money I had. I didn't know what I was going to do when I got to London. All I knew was that I'd be able to see the road more easily if Dave Stewart would stop grinning in at me through the windscreen.

III

It isn't as easy to disappear as you might think. For a start I had to find a job and to do that I needed insurance cards, and the firms generally would ask for the places I'd worked at before. The only kind of work I could do was in the electrical line and I didn't fancy answering a string of questions at some interview. Because I had so little money, the problem was urgent but I put it aside when I arrived in London and decided to concentrate on finding a flat.

That wasn't as hard as I'd expected and by Monday lunch time I was fixed up; not bad considering I didn't arrive there until six o'clock on the Monday morning.

The job was a much harder problem, but even that was solved before the end of the week. Without giving Strong's my new address I couldn't get hold of my insurance cards, so if I applied for any ordinary job, the lack of them was going to look suspicious. I spent the rest of the Monday wondering what to do about it, but it wasn't until I got Tuesday night's paper that I solved it.

I could play the piano, couldn't I? In fact, indirectly that was what had got me into the jam in the first place, so I might as well get some good out of it.

What I did was look through the adverts until I found a few pubs who wanted a pianist on different nights. I toured round

46

them and fixed up half a dozen. None of them wanted to bother with insurance cards so then I went to the civil servants and told them I was a self-employed musician who'd lost his card. They were very good to me, fixed me up with a new one, and actually credited me with the value of the stamps which I said I'd lost.

As far as I was concerned my life in Manchester was over. I didn't even write to Diane and I never heard anything more about the Fingal episode. There were a few paragraphs in the papers but they dropped it when the police made no progress in solving it, and gradually even Dave Stewart's haunting face faded away until it was just a memory, something that had happened years ago in the past.

I didn't make much from my pub playing but it was a stepping stone. The advantage was that it gave me time to build up a background with no questions asked, and gave me the contacts I needed if I was to break into the more lucrative club circuit; nine months after leaving Manchester I was making enough to move to a better flat, and a few months after that I bought an electronic organ and a new piano to replace the junky one I'd had up to then. As an organist I could double my earnings, but I much preferred the piano. The job at Meecham's was exactly what I wanted; and from it I reckoned that I could make the leap into a bigger circuit.

Things were definitely looking good.

And then Morgan Jackson turned up again.

I didn't know what this job was he had for me, but the similarity in the way he set things up frightened me. I couldn't think much about it during the rest of the evening, while I was playing, and immediately afterwards Benny Sugar, who owns the place, wanted to talk to me about some new ideas he'd had. I said I'd think about them, and by the time I'd got away, Meecham's was empty and in darkness.

I wondered a lot about it on the way home, but I got nowhere, and for the first time in twelve months I saw Dave Stewart again, in a dream. He was still grinning and he was trying to say something. When I lashed out with my fist the face flickered and split up, then the pieces gradually resembled into the face I'd seen when I'd pointed the gun at him. I woke up sweating and shivering: when I went back to sleep again, he'd gone.

The following day was Tuesday, when the

club shuts. I moped around all day not doing much. I had been intending to work on some new arrangements but I found that the thought of what Jackson might want was preying on my mind so much that I couldn't think. Eventually I gave up pretending to work and sat down with *Playboy* and a cup of coffee; at first I couldn't even concentrate on the magazine properly but a feature on go-go dancers in the States got me thinking about Vicki and for nearly an hour I forgot about Morgan Jackson.

At seven o'clock I went down to Chelsea to meet him.

It was a wet night but not cold. The windscreen wipers slapped backwards and forwards, one of them squeaking a little reminding me that I'd been meaning to replace the worn blade for the last three weeks. Because of that I couldn't see properly out of the passenger's side. I almost missed the turning into Turpin Street and caused a lot of hooting behind me by stopping suddenly. I drove along it anxiously until I came to Wagstaffe Place, and almost missed that because it wasn't what I'd been expecting.

When Jackson said it was a block of flats I'd pictured one of these modern places, similar to the one in which I lived. This one was an old house, a lord of the manor type of place which dated back to the Victorian era. I drove my car into the wide drive, past the badly painted board which said Wagstaffe Place, locked up and ran through the rain into the hall.

The house smelled faintly of disinfectant. On one of the cracked walls was a scruffy board with some names written on it with a felt pen. Mr Tagos. Miss Hansen and Miss Christien. Mr and Mrs Bean. An oddly assorted group. There was no name against the number Jackson had given me, five. I went up the stairs to the first floor and walked along a narrow passage, my feet scuffing on the bare boards. It was a gloomy derelict place and I realized now why Jackson had told me that he didn't live here. If I was meeting someone here I'd want to assure them that it wasn't my home, as well.

Flat five was right at the end of the passage, near a window which looked out at the side of the house. The rain pattered against the glass in a sharp flurry as I knocked at the door. When no one came to answer it after a couple of minutes I had a wild feeling that perhaps Jackson hadn't turned up. I dismissed it. I wasn't going to get off that easily.

I knocked again and the door creaked

slightly. Frowning, I reached out and turned the handle. The door opened easily and I stepped into the kind of room you'd expect in a house like that.

The battered, scratched furniture looked as if it had come from the nearest junk shop. A carpet from the same source once red but now a subtle shade almost verging into black. A brand new television set, shining like a jewel in a coal mine. Red curtains which weren't quite filthy enough to match the carpet and an empty bird cage, dangling from a chromium plated stand.

There was also a girl.

She would be about twenty two or three, pretty, good figure which I couldn't see properly because she was dressed for the weather in a purple maxi coat and boots, which still had glistening spots of rain on them. There was only one thing she'd done wrong when she'd been getting ready.

She'd taken the purple, floor length scarf and tied it so tightly round her neck that it had choked her.

IV

I didn't touch her. In fact for five minutes I

didn't know what I was doing. When my mind began to work again I was hunched in one of the scruffy uncomfortable chairs with my back to the girl who was lying on the rug in front of the empty fireplace. My fists were pressed to my face and clenched so tightly that when I lowered them my knuckles were white. The swine. If this was what he'd set up for me it looked as though it was all over bar waiting for the cops to walk in and find me.

When that happened, the fact that I didn't know who the girl was and that I'd never seen her before in my life wouldn't be worth a jot because scattered around would be enough evidence to convince even the most feeble minded cop that I was lying, while just to clinch things someone would phone them about the two-year-old Fingal job in Manchester.

Once they started going into that, I was finished.

Being closely involved with one murder might not prove much, but getting involved in another would be as good as a signed confession.

It all looked so obvious to me.

Too obvious, in fact.

The more I thought about it, sitting in that

pitiful room with the harsh glare of the bulb beating down on me, the more it seemed to be a curious set up. For instance, if the cops did take me in, all I had to do was start shouting about Morgan Jackson. I didn't know where he was living but if I shouted long enough and loudly enough they'd have to look for him and a lot of things would come out into the open. Seeing that Jackson had really killed the girl and I hadn't they'd be certain to find enough evidence to throw doubt on my own guilt, even if they couldn't prove anything against him.

There was another thing. He'd had to live during the past two years and there was no telling what rackets he might be connected with. The investigation might throw up something about them which could be proved.

There was no actual proof that I had been at Fingal's and shot Dave Stewart and provided I kept my head I reckoned that I could easily wriggle out of this. So there had to be something else to hold me. My previous experience had shown me that there was very little sloppy planning about Morgan Jackson's affairs and this just didn't have the right tightness. I was in a sack, all right but the mouth was open and it would be easy to crawl out. Jackson would have pulled the mouth shut, tied it with string and sewn it up, just to make sure.

I stood up. The girl's face, bloated and nearly the same shade of purple as her long coat, looked up at me. Her eyes were open but there was a shocking blankness in them, a complete absence of expression which terrified me and almost sent me back into the chair.

Carefully I walked round her to the door. It was still partly open and I closed it firmly, thankful that as this was the last door in the passage there was little chance that anyone had walked past and looked in casually. I slipped the catch on the lock so that no one could surprise me and turned back into the room.

The next part was worse. The girl was wearing gloves, and I worked them off her hands and pulled them as far onto mine as they would go. It wasn't perfect but it would stop me from leaving fingerprints all over the place. The limpness and faint warmth that was still in her told me she hadn't been dead for very long, but I wasn't expert enough to say exactly how long.

I straightened up. I didn't want to spend too long here, but before I left it was vital that I should find out whether anything had been left to implicate me.

Nothing had, so far as I could see. Not only that, but neither was there anything which could tell me who the girl was, not even a handbag. The search was made easier by the fact that as Jackson had rented this flat in a false name no one actually lived here, and all the drawers and cupboards were empty. When I was reasonably sure that there was nothing at all which would point at me I went back to the window and twitched back the curtain carefully.

There was no sign of any cops, or of anyone coming here. Two cars passed. A bus ground on its way, a pool of light in the darkness with uncaring figures looking from its windows. After a few seconds I let the curtain fall.

Either I could report it to the cops, with all that that meant, or I could go on my way and forget about it. That was the ideal thing to do but there was always the chance that Jackson had arranged something which I didn't know about, something calculated to go off if I didn't get the police, and which would pull me right into it.

That was something I would have to chance. While it wasn't certain that there was anything like that it was obvious that if I went to the police a whole lot of things were going to come out, and everything which I'd built up over the past couple of years would be smashed. And if it went I knew I would never get it back, even if I stayed out of jail.

In the end I compromised. After using the girl's gloves to wipe off any stray prints which might be around the door handle I dropped them near her body. I went downstairs, still meeting no one, and got into my car. I drove off slowly and normally, calling the cops from the next phone box I came to and hanging up before they could ask me who I was or how I came into it.

I couldn't do much for the girl but at least I could stop her from rotting in that room for a couple of weeks before anyone found her.

After that I went home, had a stiff drink and went to bed.

I slept late but when I woke I felt completely refreshed. I got the morning paper from the letter box and looked to see if there was anything in it about the girl, but there wasn't. Tossing it aside I had breakfast and then settled down to the arranging which I hadn't been able to do the day before. Ideas came easily this morning and I found that the Jackson business wasn't worrying me half as much as I'd expected.

It looked to me as though Morgan Jackson had killed the girl for some reason of his own, in which case he would probably have disappeared by now, and certainly wouldn't come bothering me any more, knowing that I must have found her and guessed what had happened. I was still bothered by the fact that he might try to throw it on me, but as it turned out I didn't have to worry for very long.

Two men called on me that afternoon.

Chief Inspector Vanning from Scotland Yard, and Sergeant Corfield.

Chapter Two

I

They nodded amiably as I let them into the flat. They didn't say anything except to introduce themselves and ask me if I was Mr Barlow; when I agreed in a harsh voice, I thought that Vanning gave me a curious look.

He was a well made, tall bloke, the kind of

person who appears in recruiting adverts to encourage people to join. He looked a typical policeman and all the time he was in the flat his eyes probed restlessly from side to side, as if they were constantly searching for evidence of something.

Maybe they were.

Corfield was quite different. Though still recognizable as a policeman he was smaller and his eyes had humorous wrinkles as if he laughed sometimes. Perhaps that's why he was still a sergeant.

To gain a little time and to cover up my anxiety and confusion I spent some minutes fussing around with sheets of manuscript paper which were scattered around, putting them into a non-existent order so that I wouldn't lose an imaginary place. When the possibilities of that were exhausted I turned back to Vanning and Corfield, much more in control of myself than I had been.

'Sorry about that,' I lied. 'Just making sure that I know where I'm up to.'

'Don't give it a thought,' Vanning said in an interested tone of voice. 'Do you compose, Mr Barlow?'

I shook my head.

'I run a jazz group at Meecham's, the club on Grundy Street. I do all the arranging for it and I sometimes do transcriptions of records for friends of mine.'

That was something I'd always done. I found it easy, especially with a solo piano record, to reproduce it after hearing it a few times; the hard slog was actually getting the notes onto paper so that other people could play it. Among my friends there was a flourishing interest in that sort of thing and I managed to do one or two good trades.

I hadn't paid the regular price for car repairs since a garage owning friend had taken up the piano, for example, and one character at a party even offered to lend me his girl friend for a week if I'd do him a transcription of a Monk long player he produced. I did the transcription but I didn't take him up on his offer.

'Very interesting,' Vanning said. 'My lad wants to be a songwriter but he can't seem to get started. Pop songs, you know the sort of thing.'

'You need a tie-in with a group for that,' I said, wishing that he'd pack this in and get to the point of why he'd come. 'None of the people likely to buy a song these days are interested in just seeing a manuscript copy of it.'

'What do they see then?'

'They don't see anything. A lot of them can't even read music. They want it on what's called a demo disc so that they can hear straight off how it sounds. It doesn't have to be a good record as such, all they're bothered about is the song, but it still costs money.'

'And you need a separate one for each song, I suppose?' he said.

I nodded.

'That's where the trouble comes, because if you don't sell any of the songs you can easily run up a big bill for no results, paying for a studio and musicians every time.'

Vanning nodded, while Corfield went over to the window and peered into the street.

'I suppose the ideal is for a budding song-writer to team up with a group that's trying to get started,' Vanning said. 'That way they can share the cost of the demo and use it to push their respective interests.'

'They can,' I agreed, 'but what happens then if neither of them get the breaks is that the group says the songs are lousy and the songwriter accuses the group of ruining his songs. And so it goes on.'

Vanning sat down on the settee and Corfield moved from the window and sat next to him, taking out an official looking notebook and a green pencil. I glanced at it but he had it open at a blank page. They seemed glad to accept the coffee which I gave them and when we were all sitting around cosily and we'd chatted some more about how crummy most modern music is and Vanning had explained that it wasn't as good as it was when he was a boy, we got down to business.

'Do you know anyone named Morgan Jackson?' he asked, putting his coffee cup and saucer down on the floor by his foot.

'I know him,' I said cautiously.

'Are you a friend of his?'

'I wouldn't say that. I know him, but that's as far as it goes.'

'When did you last see him?'

'A couple of days ago.'

'Did you see him often?'

I shook my head and tried to move my stiff lips into a smile.

'The time before that was two years ago,' I said. 'It was only by chance that I saw him the other day. He turned up in the club where I work.'

'You talked to him?'

'For about twenty minutes.'

'Did he seem worried or bothered about anything?' Vanning asked.

'Not that I could see,' I replied carefully.

'Mind you, don't forget that I hadn't seen him for two years and it probably wouldn't stand out to me if he was worried.'

'That's true,' Vanning agreed while Corfield scribbled away into his notebook. 'I don't suppose that he mentioned any of his friends, did he?'

'Not a one.'

Vanning sighed.

'I was hoping he might have done,' he said. 'I should have known better than to think I'd have it as easy as that.'

I considered that I'd waited long enough. In the pause while Corfield turned over a page of his book I looked from one to the other and then asked what the hell it was all about. I phrased it differently, of course, but that was the general sense.

'It's a very messy business and I can't see all the connections yet,' Vanning said slowly. 'In fact, there might not even be any connections. These things never do fit together as neatly as you'd like.'

'What things would those be?

'Mr Jackson was murdered last night,' Vanning said abruptly.

He couldn't have had any idea of the shock he was going to give me. Or maybe he could. He was watching me very carefully when he spoke and my hissing breath and the way I half rose in my chair seemed to reassure him that I didn't know anything about it. When I'd calmed down a little and the feeling of being hit over the head with a drum stick had died away I said:

'Now wait a minute, Mr Vanning. I don't see why you should think I know anything about that.'

'I'm not saying that you know anything about it,' he said with the smooth manner of someone who's said that to hundreds of people over the years. 'I just had information that you knew him and so I had to come round and see you, to find out if you could give me any help.'

I frowned.

'Suppose you tell me how you were so certain that I knew him. Until Monday I'd forgotten all about him. I wasn't exactly his greatest friend.'

'That's true. Miss Victoria Newnes told me.'

Victoria Newnes. Vicki, the blonde at Meecham's. I thought back and remembered how she'd come into the bar with Ray, the drummer, while I'd been talking to Morgan Jackson, but that still didn't explain anything.

'I didn't know he was a friend of Vicki's,' I

said, 'She never mentioned him afterwards.'

'This is where it starts to get messy,' Vanning said. 'You see, Miss Newnes's sister has been killed too. Apparently Mr Jackson–'

'For God's sake!' I shouted, 'What is this? I thought we were living in London, not Chicago! If there are gangsters like this roaming about it's a wonder you don't tell everyone not to go out after dark.'

He heard me out, smiling politely. When he spoke again, he had stopped talking like a human being and turned into a living police report.

'At about half past eight yesterday evening,' he said, 'a patrol car received a call to go to a building known as Wagstaffe Place, in Turpin Street, Chelsea. Wagstaffe Place is an old house which has been turned into flats. In one of the first floor flats the crew found the body of a young girl. She had been strangled with her own scarf and she was later identified from articles in her handbag which was later found thrown into some bushes in the garden.'

I listened fascinated, wondering how all the horror which I'd felt could be condensed into those few official words. Corfield had stopped writing and was looking towards the window again, as if he wanted to take another look into the street. Maybe he was afraid someone had pinched the police car and he wanted to make sure it was still there.

'We traced Kathy's sister,' Vanning went on, 'Victoria Newnes, and she said that Kathy was friendly with a man named Morgan Jackson. When we got his address and went round to see him as a matter of routine, just as we've come to see you now, we found that he was dead too.'

'How was he killed?' I asked.

'He'd been shot.'

'So where do I come in?'

'We got back to Vicki, as you call her, because she was one of the few links with Mr Jackson, and we thought she might know something else about him. She didn't but she said that you were talking to him in the bar at Meecham's on Monday night. So here we are.'

'I see,' I said. 'I'm only sorry that I can't help you more. I'm fond of Vicki and if her sister was anything like she is I'd like to think that I could help to catch whoever killed her. As I said, though, it was only by chance that I met Morgan Jackson, and I don't know a thing about him.'

Vanning nodded.

'I can see that, Mr Barlow. There's one

other question, while I'm here.'

'What's that?'

'He didn't offer you a job, by any chance?' he asked casually.

'A job? What kind of a job?' I knew that I couldn't keep some reaction out of my voice, and I tried to make it startled rather than apprehensive. 'I've got a job.'

'I realize that, Mr Barlow, but apparently he offered Kathy Newnes a job a couple of weeks ago. As far as we can gather she went to Turpin Street to meet him.'

'She didn't live there?' I asked, fishing, to try and see how much they did know.

'No,' he said, shaking his head. 'The flat was rented in the name of Jagger but so far we haven't been able to trace who that is.'

'So if she went to Turpin Street it looks as if this Jagger must have killed her,' I said, knowing that it was a false name and there was no such person. 'Find him and your problems are over.'

'It still leaves Jackson,' Vanning said. 'Don't forget she was supposed to be going there to meet him. It isn't as simple as you seem to think. What we really want is a motive for Jagger killing them both, or for Jackson killing her. He could have done, you know.'

'And you don't know what kind of a job he

wanted her to do?' I asked, torn between curiosity and not wanting to seem inquisitive.

'Not a clue,' Vanning declared. 'She worked as a model but whether he wanted her for something in that line or something entirely different, we don't know yet.' He stood up and Corfield closed his book, slipping it into his pocket.

I showed them to the door. Considering that I hadn't actually told them anything they were very grateful, but right then I couldn't have cared less about the police.

Look at it this way. Jackson had jobs to offer. He'd been killed. He'd offered one to Kathy Newnes. She'd been killed. He'd offered one to me and the next step from that was so obvious that it brought me out in a cold sweat just to think about it. I shut the door after the cops and leaned on it. My oversensitive ears listened to them going down the passage, the sound of their footsteps and the muttering rumble of voices gradually fading.

Even when they'd gone I stayed listening, and it wasn't long before I seemed to hear furtive footsteps creeping back. I let them get right up to the door and then whipped it open. There was no one in sight. I slammed it shut again, locked it and poured myself a stiff whisky. It helped, but I found myself in a panic, jumping at imaginary sounds while I tried to work out what kind of job Morgan Jackson could have had for a model and an electrician turned pianist.

After half an hour of useless wondering I picked up the phone and dialled Vicki's number. There was no answer; it didn't surprise me, for somehow I hadn't expected her to be in. After a moment's hesitation I pressed down the receiver rest, then called Benny Sugar's number.

He answered almost at once, with the nervous urgency of a man for whom telephone calls often bring important news.

He didn't sound disappointed when he realized that it was only me.

'I can guess what you're calling about,' he said as soon as he recognized my voice. 'Vicki's already been on to me and told me what's happened.'

'Did she tell you that I knew this man, Morgan Jackson?'

'She told me just about everything, I guess.' Benny comes from Norwich, and though his accent has been modified by years of living in London he still tends to sound like the Fenman when he's excited. He was excited now. 'She won't be coming in tonight, Rusty, but I'll fix up a replacement for the rest of the week. I've got a couple of girls on the list who'll be delighted to help us out.'

For once I didn't care how many girls he got.

'Is Vicki staying in London or is she going away?' I asked.

'She didn't say she was going away. All she wanted was to have the rest of the week off to get over things and deal with the police and so on. There'll be a lot for her to do. I offered to handle some of it for her but I reckon she'd rather do it herself. I found her a good lawyer to handle that side of it, but that's all.' His voice changed slightly, a note of alarm creeping into it. 'You'll be here, won't you, Rusty?'

'You could get someone off your list to replace me, couldn't you?'

'I could at a pinch, but I'd rather–'

'I'll be there as usual,' I promised and rang off.

Things were so mixed up in my mind that at first I couldn't sort myself out, but after another drink they gradually fell into a pattern.

First, and most important, if this unknown killer knew that I was involved in Jackson's job I'd be next in line for the chop. There might be other people, too, but I didn't care so much about them. The second thing was that the cops were going to do a lot of digging over this, to try and tie up some of the loose ends. If they dug far enough they were certain to come up with something about Jackson's time in Manchester, and from that they could easily start getting ideas about me and the Fingal business. I didn't see how I could prevent that but it did occur to me that I might be able to get in before them and stop a lot of harm before it started.

Not having seen Jackson for so long, there wasn't much that I knew about him and his friends. In any case, the police would be working on that, and I would only get under their feet. The only angle I had was a half forgotten name, which might not even be relevant any more.

I went into the bedroom and hefted down a small suitcase which I keep on top of the wardrobe, full of the kind of personal stuff that collects over the years. A cup final ticket from the only time I've been to Wembley. A prize I won at school, one of those ghastly books which I knew I'd never read but which I didn't like to throw away. Some sheet music that Duke Ellington once autographed for me when his band played in Manchester.

Tucked right at the bottom of the case was a battered old diary which I used as an address book. I flipped through it quickly; they were all there, from Jackson himself to Diane Thornton and a lot of other birds whom I'd long forgotten. I became so interested in trying to remember what they'd all looked like that I almost forgot what I was really after, but I found it eventually, tucked right at the back.

It was a scrap of paper that Jackson had once given me. The name and address on it were written in his square handwriting in smudged ball pen, with a neat circle for a full stop.

Steve Ashworth, a London photographer, and an address which was probably long out of date. I checked it with the phone book, found that it was still correct, and put suitcase and address book back.

There was probably nothing to it, but I remembered that at one time Jackson had been pretty friendly with this Ashworth. His name had cropped up once in a conversation we'd been having, and before I knew where I was he'd written down the address for me.

'If you ever go to London for the weekend,

boy, he's the man to see. He'll fix you up with a bird just like that, any kind you want.'

He'd leered, I'd stowed the paper away in my address book, and forgotten all about it until now.

Probably my reasoning was all screwy but as Vanning had said that Kathy Newnes was a model I didn't think it was stretching things too far to assume that she could have met Jackson through this Ashworth, either casually or professionally, as you might say. I'd have liked to have spoken to Vicki to confirm it, if I could, but she still wasn't in when I rang again, so I decided to take a chance. Even if nothing else came of it there was a chance that I'd get some other information, and with the cops poking around, and someone liable to knock me off at any minute, there was no time to lose.

I went to see Steve Ashworth.

II

The studio was nothing to shout about. Reached by a pokey, narrow doorway, it was situated on the fringe of Soho. Screwed to the door was a bright yellow sign with Ashworth's name painted on it in red, and as I stopped to read it a couple of Italians bumped into me. Without altering the rapid flow of conversation they walked round me, arms waving, greased hair flashing in the pale sunshine. I looked after them then had a look at the portraits which were in a glass case fastened to one wall; there were one or two fashion shots, too, obviously intended for the magazines, and though I'm no expert they didn't look too bad to me.

I climbed the dark flight of stairs and opened the door at the top.

It took me into a small waiting room. There was a desk in one corner with a folded back woman's magazine on it. There was a blue telephone, a blue carpet and blue curtains at the window. In a large room like this curtains looked out of place, but they did manage to add a certain badly needed tone. After standing there for a few minutes I realized that no one was going to come and see what I wanted, so I rapped sharply on the desk. Still no one came and presently I went to the multicoloured bead curtain which hung across a doorway at the back.

I rattled it to one side and looked into the next room, making sure what I was going into. It looked to be the studio itself.

Steve Ashworth would be the tall, stringy

guy with the Rollei hung around his neck. He was wearing fawn slacks and a bright blue tee-shirt. His hair was falling into his eyes and he looked warm. At the other side of the room, sitting on a wooden chair, was a he-man, male model character, with his shirtsleeves rolled up and a bored look on his face. He yawned, and then scratched his neck, and I turned my attention to the girl under the photofloods.

She really caught the eye, though she was only averagely pretty, with straight black hair and a figure which almost, but not quite, rivalled Vicki's. There was something about her, an aura which would make a fortune for the bloke who managed to capture it on film. Judging from Ashworth's set up he hadn't quite achieved it yet, and I wondered what she was doing working in these crummy surroundings.

She was wearing a pink dress and the pair of photofloods which were trained on her highlighted her make-up and made her hair glisten. Her hands were clasped beneath her chin, there was more than a hint of promise in her eyes, and the tip of her tongue poked out provocatively.

Ashworth fired off a couple of shots, leaping from one side to the other to get the best angle, then she relaxed as he lowered his camera.

'That it, Steve?' she asked.

He shook his head.

'I want to try one more before we call it a day. Simon we'll need you on this. Bring the chair over here. Carol, get your dress off love, and sit down.'

The he-man type stood up and hefted his chair into the glare of the lamps. The sight of Carol taking off her dress wiped the bored expression off his face and he looked as if he might enjoy things after all. Ashworth turned to a small desk which was pushed against the wall, and saw me.

'What do you want?' he demanded curtly. 'This is a private studio. How did you get in here?'

'There was no one to stop me,' I said mildly, 'and no one answered when I knocked on the desk so I came through.'

He frowned.

'That bloody receptionist will have to go.'

'Looks like she's gone already,' Simon said, and laughed.

'Forgetting about that, what can we do for you?' Ashworth asked. 'I can't do portraits without an appointment.'

'I don't want a portrait,' I said, moving

75

further into the room and letting the bead curtain shiver and rattle back into place. 'I want to talk to you.'

'What about?'

'They tell me you were a friend of Morgan Jackson's,' I said. I leaned against the wall while Ashworth watched me and Simon, still grinning, rested his elbows on the back of the chair.

'What about him?'

'I'd like to ask you some questions. I won't keep you more than a few minutes.'

Ashworth glanced at his watch.

'It had better not, because that's all I can spare you. I'll have to get this finished first, though. It's for a book jacket and the shots have to be in by tomorrow morning. Five minutes at the most.'

He opened a drawer in the desk, took out some lengths of thick rope and turned back to where Carol was sitting on the chair. She had on a black bra and panties. He used the rope to lash her wrists and ankles to the chair and though the knots wouldn't have held her prisoner for more than five minutes they'd look pretty good on a photograph.

'Right, Simon,' he said when he'd finished, 'stand behind her and put your hands round her neck. Carol, look as though you're being strangled by a fiend, Simon, smile for God's sake, you're supposed to be enjoying this.'

She laughed. One of the bra straps slipped off her shoulder as she wriggled. Simon clamped his hands round her neck and her face took on an expression of terror that was so real it worried me for a minute. Ashworth seemed delighted.

'That's perfect!' he cried as he shot off a couple of frames. 'Just a few more from several angles and we'll wrap it up.' He danced about the room, shooting off his camera, then eventually lowered it.

Simon began to untie Carol, and Ashworth turned to me, putting the camera on the desk.

'What do you want to ask me?'

'I'm not really sure.' I nodded towards Simon and Carol, who was getting into her dress. 'I hoped to see you alone.'

'They'll be leaving in a few minutes. You needn't worry about them.'

'I'll hang on until they've gone.'

He frowned at me.

'Maybe you'd better come into the office,' he said. 'I'm very busy, I haven't the time to play around like this.' He led the way across the studio and round a partition where there was a small office, just a desk and a couple of chairs. He offered me a chair, while he perched on the edge of the desk, which was littered with prints, negatives and boxes of chemicals.

I said: 'What I'd like to know–'

He held his hand up to stop me.

'Before I tell you anything or answer any questions I want to know who you are and why you've come here. And snap it up because–'

'Because you haven't got all day,' I broke in. 'You made that point a long time ago. My name's Barlow and I play the piano at Meecham's on Grundy Street. I've come here because I knew Jackson when he lived in Manchester and he told me that you were a friend of his.'

'Why should he say that?'

'He said that if I wanted a bird for a weekend, you were the person to get in touch with.'

'I take it you don't want a bird now?' he asked, looking at me narrowly.

Before I could answer there was a sound of soft footsteps, and a moment later Carol joined us.

'I'll see you tomorrow about those other pictures, shall I, Steve?' she asked, then winked at me. 'I should watch him,' she told me. 'You've seen what he does to defence-less girls. In front of strangers, too.' She giggled and I smiled back, still wondering what she was doing with a photographer like Ashworth.

'Suppose you get along, honey,' he said.

I watched her walk out.

'Some bird,' I said. 'I'd have her for the weekend.'

'She isn't available,' he said. 'I'm taking good care of that baby. She's going to be big in the near future and by then I'll have a lot of valuable pictures of her. Have to do it that way. She won't come near here once she hits the big time.'

Privately I didn't blame her, but I didn't say so.

'Did you see a lot of Morgan Jackson?' I asked him.

'I did at one time but I haven't seen him for four or five months. Perhaps longer. We had an argument. Just what's your interest, Barlow?'

'Jackson's dead. He was murdered last night.'

His eyes narrowed again. His head swivelled from side to side as if he was looking for a way out and his face went as white as the back of a print that was lying near his hand.

'Murdered? Who by?'

'How should I know? That's for the cops to find out.'

'Yeah. Were you a friend of his? Did you see him after he left Manchester?'

I shook my head.

'That's the trouble. Before he was killed he offered me a job and I'd like to find out what it was. There was a girl involved, too, name of Kathy Newnes.'

'Kathy?' he said, pushing his lips into a soundless whistle. 'I wouldn't have said that she was Jackson's type.'

'You know her?'

'She does work for me from time to time. Nothing regular.'

'She's dead, too.'

'Christ,' he said. 'Who's told you all this? I haven't seen anything in the papers.'

'You won't have done. The police told me because they saw me with Jackson before he was killed.' That wasn't strictly true but it was better than going into all the details. 'I was hoping that you might know what this job was.'

'I haven't a clue. Like I said, I fell out with Morgan a few months ago. What's the matter, are the cops trying to get you for it or are you worried that someone's going to knock you off too?'

'A bit of both. Knowing the tricks that Morgan got up to it struck me that any job he offered would have some good pickings and I'd like to find out the details.'

'I'll bet you would. And now that I can't tell you anything what are you going to do?'

'I've no idea,' I said frankly. 'I don't like having to let the idea drop because there's probably money in it.'

'Think that was why he was killed?'

'He could have been. You don't know who he was going around with, do you?'

'In the bird line?'

'In any line.'

He shook his head.

'We didn't talk about business because Morgan liked to keep things quiet. His women changed so quickly that I haven't a clue who he was making it with now. I didn't know anything about Kathy, for instance.'

I smiled, though I was far from having anything to smile about. As far as I was concerned the trail ended here and unless something happened to open it up again I was stuck.

Though I could always rely on the killer having a go at me, but that wasn't the kind of lead I had in mind.

'I'm sorry,' Ashworth said, 'but I don't think there's much I can help you with.'

I stood up. There was no point in staying here any longer. I pushed the chair away and went round the partition again, back in to the studio. Simon and Carol had both left and it was empty.

'I'm sorry,' Ashworth repeated as I went out through the bead curtain. 'I'd really like to help you.'

'I'm sure you would.' There was still no sign of the receptionist, though the magazine had gone. On impulse I handed him one of my cards. 'Maybe you'll give me a ring if you hear anything.'

'Yeah,' he said imitating my own earlier manner. 'I'll do that. So long.'

III

As it was nearly tea-time by then I wondered whether to go home or not, then slipped into a cafe on Oxford Street where I could eat without being disturbed. I had tea as quickly as the waiters would permit, then went to a phone booth. This time Vicki answered the third ring.

'Hi, Vicki,' I said. 'Can I come round and see you?' There were still two hours before I was due at Meecham's.

'If you want.' She sounded listless and bemused, and I wasn't surprised. I didn't talk much over the phone and it took me about half an hour to get to her flat which wasn't too far away from Turpin Street.

I'd been here once or twice before, on the occasions when her car was in for servicing and I'd given her a lift home from Meecham's. It was an averagely smart place, not dingy like a lot of flats I've been in, but nothing to scream about either. I went up the stairs and rang the bell. There was a short delay before she answered it and stood back to let me in.

'I'm sorry–' we both began together, then stopped.

She gave a weak smile.

'Go on,' I said. 'Ladies first.'

She didn't speak right away but led me into the lounge. Her dancing costume was lying on the settee, with a needle threaded with white cotton stuck in it. She picked it up, folded it, put it in a cupboard and turned back to me.

'Drink?' she asked.

'I'll get them,' I said. 'I know where

83

everything is. You sit down and say what you started to say when you let me in.'

'I'm sorry I had to send the police round without warning you,' she said, still in the dazed tone of voice. She dropped into one of the armchairs and smoothed her dress. 'I don't know what I'm doing, Rusty, everything seems in a whirl.'

'I shouldn't worry about it,' I said. 'I was sorry to hear about Kathy.' We exchanged conventional remarks for a minute or two and then I said: 'Vanning told me that Jackson had offered Kathy a job.'

'That's right. I didn't know much about him, actually. She had her own flat about a mile from here and the only time I saw him was about three weeks ago.' She looked at me over the top of her glass. 'I didn't like him very much, Rusty.'

'Don't mind me,' I said. 'He wasn't a friend of mine.'

'But I thought—'

'You thought he was when you saw us together the other night?' I shook my head. 'I knew him before I came to live in London and I only met him by chance on Monday. I didn't like him too much before, and he hadn't improved with the keeping, but you know how it is when you see someone you used to work with. You feel bound to have a word with them.'

She nodded.

'Any idea how Kathy met him?' I asked.

'I haven't a clue. She was a model, you know, and she was involved with a lot of queer characters, photographers and the like. She could have met him through one of them.'

'What I'm worried about,' I said, sipping my drink, 'is this. Jackson was going about offering jobs to people. He's dead now and so is one of the people he offered a job.'

'So?'

'He told me he had just the job for me, too.'

She took a second or two to get the point of that. When it clicked she drew in her breath sharply and opened her eyes very wide.

'Have you told the police about this?' she demanded. 'I mean, if someone's going to kill you because of something Jackson said they ought to do something about it. They should protect you, at least.'

'I haven't mentioned it to them. I don't think I'd care to be watched all the time by a couple of cops, and in any case they've more important things to do than look after me. What I would like to know is what these jobs were. Must be something pretty explosive.'

Her legs were fine, dancer's legs, a little heavy because of all the strength that had been packed into them but none the worse for that. She tucked them underneath her on the chair, then shook her head.

'She didn't tell me what kind of a job it was and to tell you the truth I don't think she really knew herself.'

'How did you hear of it?'

'It was that time I went to her flat and saw Jackson. He left soon after I arrived and when he'd gone I asked her who he was.' She smiled. 'You know what it's like. He looked too old to be her boy friend, and in any case he wasn't her type. I was curious.'

'And what did she say?'

She finished off her drink and sat twisting the glass round between her fingers. Comparing her with the happy, carefree Vicki I was used to, it was easy to see the marks of strain on her face and the dullness of her eyes. She was wise to take a few days off and even if she hadn't wanted to I think Benny would have done his best to change her mind.

'She didn't say much except that his name was Morgan Jackson and that he'd offered her a job,' she told me, still turning the glass round. 'We started talking about him and how she'd met him through some other friends but when I got round to asking her about the job she said she didn't know what it was all about because he hadn't told her yet. We took it that it would be something to do with modelling.'

'She'd done that for a long time, had she?'

'A couple of years. She did pretty well out of it, too. She started about the same time I went to Paris as a dancer.'

'Did she have many boy friends?'

'A lot. No one special.' She looked at me a little oddly. 'Just what are you trying to do, Rusty? You sound like that man Vanning.'

'I'm sorry. All I want to know is whether anyone's likely to take a crack at me. If I knew what these secret jobs were that Jackson was hawking around I might get a bit nearer.'

And, I thought, there was the question of what the cops were likely to dig up about me when they enquired into Jackson's past.

'Why don't you leave things like that to the police?'

'It intrigues me. If you were in my position, you'd be intrigued, too.'

'I suppose I would,' she said slowly. 'It all seems very dangerous to me. I mean, look what's happened already.'

'That's what I'm afraid of, Vicki,' I said. 'Are you sure that Kathy hasn't said anything else that might help me?'

She thought about it. I could see that she was really thinking and not just pretending and after a moment or two she said hesitantly:

'There is one thing. It might be nothing to do with it, but I thought it was queer at the time and I'm sure that it was Jackson she was talking to.'

'What's that?'

'Last week I went round to see her. I hadn't been there long when the phone rang. There was nothing definite but I got the impression she was trying to choke the caller off, as if she didn't want to say too much while I was there. The more I think about it, the more I'm sure that she was speaking to Morgan Jackson.'

'How do you know that?'

She put the glass on the floor.

'He was talking very loudly. I could hear his voice and I could make out a little of what he was saying. I heard him say to her: "You've no money now but the Yanithos Collection will change all that." He rang off then.'

'The Yanithos Collection?' I said, frowning. 'A queer name. What the devil is it?'

'I've no idea. I was a bit put out because I thought that it was something she didn't want me to know about, so I didn't ask her.'

I hesitated.

'Was she short of money?' I said. 'Or is that a question I shouldn't ask?'

'Ask what you want,' she said with a shrug. 'I don't really know how much she had but I wouldn't have said that she was short. Not if the rate she spent it is anything to go by, that is.'

There didn't seem too much for me there, though it was interesting to see Vicki falling into the same trap as a lot of people. Just because a person spends a lot doesn't mean that they've got a lot. Look at me with Diane Thornton, when I had been spending so much that I'd had to go to moneylenders like Deany to keep it up. For all we knew, Kathy could have been up to the hilt with a gang of moneyboys, and that could have something to do with her death.

Certainly it stank of Jackson's technique.

Getting himself killed too was the odd thing which didn't fit in.

Vicki was looking at me hopefully, as though she thought I might have made some useful suggestion. If she was expecting that, I'm afraid I must have disappointed her.

'What did Vanning tell you he was going to do?' I asked.

'He didn't say. I had to give him your name as soon as he started talking about Morgan Jackson and he said he'd see you. That was about all. And he took the names of as many of Kathy's boy friends as I could remember. There was an address book at her flat, so he'll be working through that, too.'

Which would mean that he'd get round to Ashworth eventually. As she'd worked for him, his name was certain to be in it. As long as Ashworth didn't say that I'd been round asking questions I'd be all right.

'Did you tell him about the Yanithos Collection?' I asked Vicki.

She shook her head.

'It didn't occur to me. I suppose I was too dazed by the fact that Kathy was dead to think about it. Do you think I should ring him up and tell him now?'

'I wouldn't. It's probably nothing to do with it and it'll only start him off on a lot of other tiresome questions. If there is anything in it you can bet that the cops will turn it up for themselves.'

'I suppose they will.' She glanced at a small silver clock which stood over the fireplace. 'I don't want to seem as if I'm rushing you off but shouldn't you be going to Meecham's soon? I've told Benny that I'm not going in for the rest of the week.'

I nodded.

'I'll get off now. I spoke to him earlier on the phone and he said he was going to get some kid off that list he has of young hopefuls. I'll bet she isn't as good as you.'

She smiled at me.

'It's nice of you to try and cheer me up,' she said. 'Rusty, don't do anything silly and get yourself hurt, will you?'

There was something in her eyes which I've never seen before, a mixture of concern and interest. It startled me, and I didn't quite know how to deal with it. Since Diane Thornton I'd been wary of getting too involved with girls, though Vicki might be different; or there could be nothing in it, of course, and it was just reaction, or my imagination.

'I'll take care,' I promised. 'Just as long as no one tries to kill me.'

I went down the stairs, trying to make what I could of the information which Vicki had given me.

The Yanithos Collection, whatever it might be, was the interesting part. I should have to find out something about it but I didn't want to go around asking too many clumsy questions in case it was something which would drag me into further trouble with the police.

I was cutting things very fine now, but there was just time to get to my flat, grab some music which I needed and get back to Meecham's before Benny started having a fit. I was lucky with the Tube trains, and reached home with a few minutes to spare. On the way I'd kept a wary eye open for anyone who might be trying to kill me, but I saw no one suspicious. There wasn't a soul in the passage, either, and no sign that the front door lock had been tampered with.

I shoved in my key and turned it.

As I did so, I heard the phone start to ring.

I let it ring as I shut the door, locked it, then took a quick peep to make sure that no one was waiting to welcome me.

I shook myself irritably. If this started to get a habit I wouldn't be able to do a thing without looking over my shoulder first to make sure that no one was waiting with a knife.

That damned phone was annoying me with its constant noise, and though I couldn't really afford the time I went over to it and plucked the receiver off.

'Hello,' I snapped.

'Is that Rusty Barlow?' a voice asked.

It was a rave from the grave or a blast from the past, whichever you like to call it. I hadn't heard from her for over two years, but there was no mistaking that voice.

It belonged to Diane Thornton.

Chapter Three

I

'What's the matter, Rusty?' she asked softly, after I'd been silent for a couple of minutes. 'You haven't been struck dumb have you?'

I took a grip on myself and tried to get my breathing under control again. I was taking short gasps, and my heart was beating so loudly that I was sure she must be able to hear it over the phone.

'No,' I said, 'I haven't been struck dumb. I'm just waiting a minute so that I don't say something I might regret.'

She laughed, and I could picture her as she had been two years ago, laughing like that on the settee at my flat. There was a gesture that went with it, a movement of her head and an impulsive touch on my arm. At one time it had made me somersault through hoops, but not now. Now, it was just a noise and meant that she wanted something off me.

'Look, Diane,' I said, 'if you've got something to say, let's hear it. I've got work to do, a job to go to, and I should be setting off any time now.'

'Of course. They tell me you're playing piano at Meecham's now. I haven't heard you there but you must be pretty good to have got so far.'

'Who told you that?' I asked sharply.

'Morgan Jackson.'

'I always thought you were working for him in the old days,' I said slowly. 'Do you mean you were still seeing him?'

'Why not? Morgan and I were the best of friends until he was killed.' Her voice hardened. 'That brings me to why I rang you up, Rusty. I reckon that you ought to come round and see me.'

'Why should I?'

'Don't forget that Morgan told me a lot, Rusty. I know all about Fingal's and why you left Manchester. What was his name? Dave Stewart?

I should have expected that but I hadn't. It caught me where it hurt and I realized that I was in a far greater jam than I'd thought. I gripped the receiver very hard, then released it slowly and said:

'What do you want to see me about?'

'I can't tell you that over the phone Rusty. You should know better than that.'

'You only want to see me because you want something off me. You think that if you're there in person it'll be easier to get me to agree. On the phone I can always hang up if I get too bored.'

'Rusty,' she said softly, 'if I want you to agree to anything I've got better ways of doing it. I just want to see you. There are things we've got to talk about.'

With all the gen about Fingal's up her sleeve I suppose she could have spun a good line in persuasion if she'd wanted. There was something else that might be useful, though; if she had been that close to Morgan Jackson it was likely that she knew all about this job.

'When had you in mind that I should come?' I asked, with one eye on the clock.

'Tonight?' she suggested.

'Don't forget that I'm playing at Meecham's until half past eleven.'

95

'Come then,' she said. 'This is urgent, Rusty.'

'It sounds like it. Where are you living now?'

She gave me an address, then hung up without saying anything else. I put my phone down slowly, trying to see all the new complications which had been introduced, but after a minute or two I gave up. There were too many of them, and the only thing to do was meet them as they came.

I didn't play well at Meecham's that night. For a start I was late and as I slid onto the stool only about five minutes before we were due to begin Ray tapped his bass drum lightly.

'Don't bother to turn up now that Vicki isn't here, eh? We can see what the attraction is, can't we?'

Tex, on the guitar, laughed. Pamela, Vicki's dancing companion, looked at me as though this business had dulled her already sluggish mind. Before I could reply the curtains swung back and as I played the opening notes I heard Ray say:

'Don't worry. Leena will look after you.'

Leena was the girl who'd replaced Vicki for the rest of the week, a blonde Swede who couldn't really dance, but as she laughed a lot between numbers we had a jolly time. In spite of my playing, which to me sounded awful, the punters seemed pleased, and that meant Benny Sugar would be pleased as well.

As I was leaving he called me into his office.

'Did you know Morgan Jackson well?' he asked after the conventional preamble about what a shock it all was, especially for young Vicki.

'Not really. I saw him on Monday night but that was the first time in two years. He was someone I used to work with in Manchester.'

Benny is middle-aged and went bald a long time ago. He's also fat and overflows the swivel chair in his office. He doesn't look the slightest bit comfortable, the way he sprawls in it but I suppose he must be or he wouldn't do it. Being so much older than the girls like Vicki he tends to keep a fatherly eye on them, making sure that they're well looked after and none of the customers get too fresh. He relies on me for a lot of the gossip he picks up, but there was nothing to tell him that night.

Faintly we could hear the voice of Mad Mike, the disc jockey, who plays on for another hour after I've gone home. He was socking it through the amplifiers as he introduced the latest hit sensations, Myriad Guests, a group which was going to be around for a long time, to judge from the musical press; in the fast moving pop world where these people come and go like snowballs dropped into a fire that meant all of a couple of months. Not my scene.

It was about quarter to twelve by the time I escaped from Benny and drove to the address that Diane had given me. It was one of those lush, Mayfair places, but that didn't surprise me. Slumming was never one of Diane's habits. After asking a uniformed porter for directions I went up in a silent lift. The place was so high class that he didn't bat an eyelid at my going up to see her at this time; anywhere else, even if there'd been a night porter, I'd have got a knowing smile, at least.

The bell bonged softly when I pressed the white push on the door. She didn't hurry about opening it but when she did there was no fumbling about, no hesitancy about whether it might be me or some more dodgy character.

'Leslie on the desk phoned to say you were on your way up,' she explained as she showed me in. 'I told him I was expecting you about this time.'

She had changed less than I'd expected. A slight fattening around the face was the most obvious thing. The same superb figure, the same polished gold hair, the same way of walking and moving that made men's tongues hang out when they saw her. She was wearing a simply cut white dress with a single rope of pearls round her neck. I reckoned that to pay for dress and pearls I'd have to work for six months at Meecham's and save every penny.

Her voice showed more change. When I'd first known her she'd been like me, with a Northern accent. Living in the South had started to erode even mine, but hers had changed completely. To hear her speak now you'd think that she'd been born at the moated manor hall, instead of a two up, two down council house.

'Sit down,' she said. 'A drink?'

I sat down, swallowed and looked at my feet to reassure myself that they were still there and hadn't been lost under all that carpet. She went over to a softly lit cocktail cabinet, mixed a couple of drinks and after handing me one sat down in a chair opposite.

'It's been a long time, Rusty,' she said, smoothing her dress. 'You never even said goodbye, either.'

'After what you'd done, did you expect me to?' I asked roughly. 'If you start that caper you'll have me in tears.'

'Of laughter?' she asked. 'Did you know that I was working with Jackson in those days?'

'I guessed it afterwards. It wasn't too hard. Did you pick on me deliberately?'

She shook her head. Her hair brushed her shoulders lightly and gleamed in the light.

'It was just chance, after that party. As soon as I found out where you worked I realized how useful you could be, and told Jackson. From then on, it was simple.'

I took a sip of the drink. It was a smooth whisky with a bite to it that made Meecham's stuff taste like water.

'Tell me,' I said, fascinated by her voice, 'do you always talk like that or are you just putting it on for my benefit?'

'It's all part of the equipment,' she replied. 'To get where I've got in the last two years you've got to know what you're doing. The people Jackson and I have been mixing with don't want a girl around who sounds as if she's dropped in by mistake.'

'Morgan Jackson pays for all this, does he?' I laughed. 'Silly question. You don't pay

100

for anything yourself, do you, Diane?'

'Why should I?' she asked reasonably, and laughed. That hadn't changed a bit and the sound and gestures brought back so many memories that I had to look away so that she wouldn't see the subtle effect she was starting to have on me.

The blank face of a colour television stared at me. To one side of it was a polished table with a glass figure of a woman on it, about four inches high. I don't go much for stuff like that normally, but that one certainly caught my eye. There was something about it which showed me how much it must have cost, a sort of living quality, as if it were looking straight at me and the smile on its face was just for me. With an effort I dragged my eyes away from it and turned back to Diane.

She was watching me with a quiet smile on her face.

'What exactly have you been doing since I saw you last?' I asked, feeling stupid.

'This and that,' she said lightly, obviously not intending to tell a thing that she didn't have to. 'I've managed to work my way up to this, and I don't suppose that I shall stop here, either.'

I shrugged.

'Rusty,' she said sharply, 'I think it's time we stopped fencing with each other and got down to business. How much did Morgan tell you?'

'What about?'

'Anything.'

'Not much,' I said vaguely, hoping to draw her out a little more.

She pressed her lips together. I could tell that she'd been expecting me to be as pliable as I'd been in Manchester, and she hadn't realized that other people could change, just like she had herself.

'You must have talked about something when he saw you,' she said eventually. 'What was it?'

'This and that. He didn't mention your name, if that's what you're after. I thought he was just small time and you'd have split with him long ago.'

'Don't you believe it,' she said. 'Did he say anything about a job?'

'A little. Why?'

'I just wondered.'

'Diane,' I said, 'maybe I'm older and sharper than I was up North or maybe easy living has softened your brain a trifle. When you worked that stunt to get me in Jackson's clutches I never suspected a thing, but

102

you're playing this so badly, it stinks.'

She ran her tongue over her lips, then took a sip of her drink. I noticed that her hands were trembling very slightly.

'Why don't you admit that there's some crook plan I was supposed to be dragged into?' I went on, 'and now that Jackson's dead you want to know how much he told me and where you stand.'

'Wouldn't you feel the same, in my position?'

'Probably, if I was stupid enough to get into it in the first place.'

'You were stupid enough before,' she flared.

I waved my arm easily. I was starting to enjoy this, and I could see that she was nowhere near as confident as she had been on the phone.

'I was younger, and I've learned a lot since then. What's the racket?'

She shook her head.

'It's no use asking me that because I don't know.'

'Don't give me that.'

'It's the truth. I'll tell you but I wouldn't say it to anyone else.' She leaned over, touching my arm lightly. 'Why don't we stop this scrapping, Rusty? It isn't doing any good. Either tell me how much you know or all that information about what you did at Fingal's will be sent to the police.'

'And suppose I tell them all about you?'

She laughed again and finished off her drink.

'What about me?' she asked. 'What have I done to interest the police? I haven't killed anyone.'

Something about the sneering way in which she said that got me. I half rose but she just stayed where she was, smiling at me calmly. After a moment I flopped back into the chair and rubbed my hand over my face. She was right, of course, and however much I tried to bluster I couldn't alter it. There was probably nothing which could be traced directly to her and by mentioning her name to the cops all I'd be doing would be digging a deeper hole for myself and giving her chance to make a fool of me. All she'd have to do would be to tell Vanning that I'd made a pass at her and this was my way of getting my own back because she'd ignored me.

'Jackson didn't tell me anything,' I said wearily. 'He said that he had a job for me and if I didn't play he'd tell the cops about me. I arranged to meet him at Turpin Street. When I got there I found a dead girl. I tipped off the cops without giving them my name, and

I only found out later who she was.'

'You didn't know at the time?'

'I'd never seen her before. As luck would have it, the dead girl's sister had seen me talking to Jackson the day before, and knew who he was.'

'How?' she asked sharply.

'I don't know. I didn't go into it in every tiny detail.' I wasn't going to involve Vicki if I could help it; the last thing I wanted was these two meeting. 'I suppose she'd seen them together or something. When I spoke to her she didn't seem to know anything more than that.'

She looked relieved.

'And what do the police think?' she asked.

'You mean you don't know?' I said, surprised.

She hesitated, fiddling with the empty glass, turning it round and round. After a moment she looked at me from under her lashes and said:

'Morgan didn't live here, Rusty. He had his own flat.'

'So?' I asked, still baffled, then suddenly it struck me what a jam she was in, and I smiled.

She watched me.

I said: 'So there's nothing to connect you

with Jackson? The police won't come here because they don't know you knew him. Is that it?'

'You must see what a mess I'm in!' she said, her voice rising, though her new accent didn't even tremble. 'Someone's killed him. I don't know who it was and I don't even know who he was working with.'

'Didn't he tell you?

'No. He said it was so there was no chance that I'd get involved with the police.'

'But now you want to know what they're likely to find out, and whether the people who killed Morgan Jackson are likely to come and kill you? You've no ideas who it might be?'

'None at all,' she said, obviously making an effort to keep her voice down. 'There was a big job coming off, that's all I know. I can't even tell you who he was working with on that.'

'He told you that I was involved, did he?'
She nodded.

'He found out that you were working at Meecham's and he told me he could use you. He was delighted about it.'

'You don't know how he wanted to use me?'

'No.'

106

'How did he come to see me at Meecham's? Was that just chance or did someone tip him off?

'I don't know.'

'For someone who was so close to Jackson you don't know much, do you?' I asked with a frown. 'He kept you in a place like this, yet he wouldn't tell you anything. That doesn't add up to me. How did you know that he was dead?'

'He went off to see you at Meecham's,' she said, 'and that was the last time I saw him. One of his friends rang me up early this morning and told me that he was dead.' She swallowed. 'I thought you might have killed him.'

'How do you know I haven't?'

'I don't, but I think that there could be someone else.'

'Someone interested in the same job and knocking off Jackson's mob one at a time?' I asked. 'And you don't know who or what the police are doing about it. That's sweet, isn't it?'

'It's not funny,' she said sharply.

'You've no idea how funny it is to me,' I told her. 'Now that you've found out how little I know, what are you going to do?'

She didn't answer right away. To give

herself time to think she went over to the cocktail cabinet and mixed some more drinks. When she sat down again it was next to me on the settee. I moved away from her but I could still smell her perfume and feel the warmth of her near me.

'The old tricks don't work, Diane,' I said.

'You never know,' she said, giving me that look from underneath her lashes again.

'I'm damned certain.' I had a drink of whisky and changed the subject. 'You say that you know all about Dave Stewart and Fingal's. How many of your pals have you told about it?'

'Not a one,' she replied after a moment.

'So what's to stop me from squeezing your rotten little neck, going home and forgetting all about it?'

'Leslie on the desk downstairs knows that you were coming here. He couldn't do anything about Fingal's but he could tell the police you were here tonight. Kill me if you want, but once they started to question him you'd be finished.'

'Jackson might not have told you much about what he was up to, but he's certainly trained you well,' I said. 'What do you want me to do?'

'Forget all about it,' she said. 'Whatever

Morgan wanted you to do doesn't exist any more. The only interest you'll have from now on is that you'll phone me every time the police come to see you and you'll tell me what they're doing. In return, I'll keep quiet about Fingal's.'

'A good bargain on your part, but don't forget that you can't prove Fingal's.'

She laughed.

'That doesn't work, Rusty. The police will still have a complete file of information on it and once they realize that you're the same Rusty Barlow who disappeared then they'll start wondering how you come to be involved in another murder. They won't take long after that.'

'And what do I do if someone tries to kill me because they think that I'm one of Jackson's gang?'

'Have they tried yet?'

'Not that I've noticed.'

She turned her glass round slowly, so that the light sparkled on it. Across the room, the glass figure smiled at us. I stared at it without smiling back.

Diane said: 'From the speed they moved with Morgan and Kathy I think they'd have killed you at the same time if they'd known you were involved. If they haven't even tried it means you're safe because they don't know anything about you.'

That sounded sensible and put like that it was just a problem for Diane, while I forgot all about it. On the other hand she knew about Fingal's and as soon as she wanted some legwork doing the pressure would come on, doubled this time because it wouldn't be too hard to finger me for killing Jackson and Kathy Newnes. Whatever I did, I was still in a jam and I wasn't falling for any line of hers.

From the way she was watching me I could tell that she knew what I was working out.

'It won't be like that, Rusty,' she said impulsively.

'Won't it?' I said bitterly. 'It's been like that in the past and I can't see any reason why things should change. Can you?'

'Promise,' she said, like a schoolkid.

I laughed.

'So I gamble my freedom on one of your promises, do I? Not likely. I've fallen for that line before. And don't forget that I know a lot about alarm circuits, my love, and that's valuable knowledge to the kind of friends you're likely to have. It's worth five hundred quid, or even a thousand on a big job, I should imagine. Why should they buy it when they can put pressure on me and get it for free, any time they want?'

She giggled.

'It sounds like the actress and the bishop,' she said.

'Maybe it does,' I said impatiently, 'but it doesn't alter the facts. How did Jackson get all this dough anyway? What was his racket?'

She hesitated, then leaned back, crossing her legs.

'I don't suppose it'll do any harm telling you now. The whole things fallen apart anyway. He was an astrologer.'

'A what?

'An astrologer.'

'Seriously?'

She nodded.

'Your fortune in the stars,' I said. 'You mean that he's made all this money by getting hold of suckers and making them think he can tell the future?'

'You'd be surprised how gullible people are,' she said. 'Especially if there's a lot of atmosphere, technical sounding stuff that doesn't really mean anything thrown at them, that sort of thing.'

'I suppose it could work, especially with a place like this and a bird like you to lush them up first.'

I was starting to see just what value Diane would have had to Jackson. It was the same principle they'd used on me; mugs would fall for a smooth line from her far more easily than they would from him, especially the men. In a racket like that, he'd be certain to get hold of a lot of secrets, too, on the pretext that clients weren't supposed to hide anything from him; handled properly, it could be worth several hundred quid a month to him, probably more if he organized it well enough.

Knowing Jackson he'd have it all organized down to the last star, and from the state of this flat he didn't look to have been short of a few quid.

'Did he use any other girls besides you?' I asked.

'Sometimes.'

'Know any of their names? Was Kathy one of them?'

'Maybe. That was business. I usually kept out of it.'

'How about a photographer called Steve Ashworth? Why did Jackson fall out with him?'

'Rusty, I don't know. There was some sort of an argument but I didn't go into it. I never did like Ashworth much. He was always getting the wrong ideas.'

I grinned to myself. Right now he was probably getting the wrong idea about that girl Carol who'd been there when I'd called, trying to get what he could off her before her career outgrew him.

'What about the Yanithos Collection?' I asked. 'Where does that come in? Or is that something else that you've never heard of?'

'The what?' From the look in her eyes I could tell that she was as much in the dark as me about that, even if she had been lying before.

'Skip it,' I told her. 'It's something that I happened to hear about.'

She stood up suddenly and banged her glass down on top of the cocktail cabinet, so hard that the bottles inside shivered together with a faint tinkling sound, although nothing broke.

'Rusty,' she said, 'I've tried to put it to you gently but you won't take any notice. Either you can stop poking your nose into this or you'll be fingered to the police. Think about it and let me know in the morning. You'll find the phone number in the book.'

And that was that. I left then, at about a quarter past one. The night was chilly and I was glad when I was in the car again with the heater turned up. I drove in a kind of dream and it was a wonder that I didn't hit something and kill myself. Maybe it would have been better if I had; far from solving any problems, Morgan Jackson's death seemed to have done nothing but create more. With all the talk about the past I saw something that I had forgotten for a long time.

Dave Stewart was laughing at me through the windscreen, just as he's been when I set off for London after the robbery.

I concentrated on the road, trying to shut him out, but he was on the edge of my mind all the time. When I eventually reached home I was something of a wreck, what with having been on the go since early morning, and all the shocks on top of it. I left the car, and went up to my flat, glad to be home, where I could go to sleep and forget about everything for a few hours.

I was so bemused that I forgot to take the precaution of checking that it was safe before I went in. I unlocked the door, walked in and slammed it shut. Hardly stopping in the hall I went through into the living room and reached up to snap on the light.

Before my fingers touched the switch I sensed a blow crashing towards my head.

II

I don't know how I avoided having my head smashed open. As I had just come into the dark room from the well lighted passage I couldn't see properly and when I heard the faint swish which preceded the blow I simply flung myself to one side. For all I knew I might have been jumping into another attacker, but there was no time to make sure.

Something whipped past my head. Then I hit the floor with a thud which knocked all the breath out of me. As I lay recovering I heard a grunt from near the door, as if my attacker had recovered his balance and was shaping up for another go.

By now, my eyes were becoming accustomed to the darkness and as long as the light was off I had a slight advantage. I was familiar with the layout of the flat and my attacker wasn't, even if he'd had a look round before I came in.

As he rushed at me I scrambled to my feet. He was a big guy, his body just a dark shape, and as he came nearer he seemed to give the illusion that he was swelling up even more. I waited, crouching, fully awake now and ready for whatever he tried next.

He swung a punch at my head. I ducked. His other fist came up and hit my chin, snapping my head back and nearly lifting me off the ground. I felt myself falling again but this time there was a muzziness about my brain that hadn't been there before, and a temptation to sink down and forget about everything. I struggled to keep conscious. My mind might have been dazed but it wasn't as bad as all that. It knew that if I lay down I'd never get up again.

He came in fast for the attack. I grabbed at his legs and pulled, using his own weight to throw him over. As he hit the floor I scrambled onto him and thrust my fingers into his thick mop of hair.

'All right,' I said, gasping for breath, my own hair in my eyes so that I could barely see, 'what are you after?'

He didn't speak. I banged his head down on the carpet and made him grunt.

'Let's have it,' I said. 'Who sent you here?'

He jerked up and down like a landed fish before you hit it with the gaff. He was so violent that I was almost thrown off, but I stopped him by rapping his head on the floor again. His arm patted around the carpet and suddenly came up so fast that I almost missed it. Luckily he hadn't time to aim the blow properly, because he was holding a short, poker affair, the thing he must have tried to hit me with as I came in. It whistled past my head and filled me with a savage fear, a strange feeling of breath-lessness that seemed to freeze my brain.

That thing could kill.

I grabbed for his arm, caught it and twisted. Because of the way he was lying I was slightly off balance and he suddenly rolled to one side. Helpless to prevent it, I was pulled over with him. I felt his breath on my ear, then we were struggling again. We rolled about the floor for what seemed like half the night but which couldn't have been more than a minute or two. I grabbed his ear. He caught my wrist between his hands and crushed it. As I let go his ear he scrambled away from me, getting to his feet.

The poker was lying around somewhere.

I didn't know where it was, but if he did, I was sunk.

During this brawl we had been making a hell of a lot of row. The time was about quarter to two and the part of my mind that wasn't thinking about the thug was wondering when someone else was going to start complaining, and come to see what was going on. No one was there at the moment and I drove him back towards the door with a series of short, savage blows. He put his hands up to protect himself, then backed into the wall.

I heard him groan.

'It's a pity you didn't kill me when I came in,' I said breathlessly. 'If you'd killed me then, you'd have got away with it, wouldn't you?'

He didn't say anything. I reached up to switch on the light so I could get a good look at him. For a second or two my attention was off him, and he wasn't as beat as I'd thought. He punched me in the face, whipped the door open with his other hand, and dashed out into the passage.

I snapped on the light.

All I got was a quick glimpse of his face, fatter than I'd thought it was, with thick lips and a flat, broad nose. No one could have called him handsome but in his trade looks aren't something that people keep for long. That's assuming they start with them, and he hadn't.

I ran after him. He was halfway towards the stairs by the time I got into the passage but there was a chance that I could catch him before he got into the street. More than anything I wanted to know who'd sent him; if he got away there was no telling when another attack might come.

'Mr Barlow!' a curt voice said behind me. I looked over my shoulder. The guy standing there was a thin, bald headed punk who lives in the flat above mine. He must have heard the row and come down the back stairs to see what was happening. His name was Wheeler and of all the people who could have complained I wasn't surprised that he was the one who'd actually done it.

'Back in a minute,' I told him and ran off.

'If this noise doesn't cease I shall call the police,' he said in his reedy voice.

That brought me up short. The cops were the last people I wanted, even though I had nearly been killed. I turned back to him, pushing the hair out of my eyes and smiling.

He looked at me with disfavour.

'When you've finished your drunken revels, maybe we can all go back to sleep,' he said nastily. 'Some of us have jobs to go to in the morning, if you haven't.'

'Yeah,' I said, 'I've finished now. You'd better get back to sleep right away.'

He pressed his lips together.

'I don't think–' he began, and then his voice was cut off abruptly as I went back into my flat and shut the door on him. It didn't worry me what he thought. The only thing that worried me now was who had sent that character to kill me, and Wheeler had effectively stopped me from finding out. A vision of him as the master crook, giving orders in that reedy, grating voice of his, actually made me smile, then I poured myself a stiff drink and sat down.

The poker that the thug had used was at the far side of the room, a short steel rod about half an inch round, and a foot long. One blow from that would have seen off anyone and I started to sweat as I realized how lucky I'd been. Gradually the whisky worked its soothing magic and I started to feel more relaxed. I sat there for a quarter of an hour then stood up to go to bed. My wrist was sore where it had been squeezed between those giant hands, but apart from that there was nothing wrong with me and inside ten minutes I was asleep.

It's a funny thing but when I woke in the morning a lot of stuff which had been puzzling me the night before was clear in my mind. I lay in bed for ten minutes or so, working out the details, getting everything clear, then I dressed and had breakfast. I use the term morning loosely; it was actually nearly eleven o'clock, but it's nothing new for me to be getting up at that time.

After breakfast I grabbed the phone book and turned up Diane's number. After I had dialled it there was a longish wait before she answered. When she spoke, her voice sounded sleepy. As soon as she realized who was calling she snapped out of it.

'Why, Rusty,' she exclaimed. 'Have you thought about what we were saying last night?'

'I've thought about it.'

'And what have you decided?' She was almost purring, so certain was she of what I was going to say.

'You set me up pretty smartly, didn't you? Just like the old days.'

'What do you mean?'

'Aren't you surprised to hear from me? Or did he tell you what happened?'

'Did who tell me what?' she asked, a note of caution creeping into her voice. 'I don't know what you're talking about.'

'Listen, kid,' I said, 'all you wanted from me last night was to find out how much I know, how much Jackson told me about your filthy plans. When you realized that I don't know a thing you let me get away and had that thug try to kill me.'

'I don't–'

'How did he get here in time?' I went on. 'Was he waiting here while I was talking to you? Did you give him a ring as soon as I left your place to tell him to either get the hell out of it or kill me? Is that it? Or would he have killed me whatever I'd said?'

She laughed. It was a nervous laugh but I could see that she was recovering from her surprise and thinking of the things she could say to me.

'I don't know who Jackson was working with so I can't speak for them, but I certainly don't want to kill you,' she said. 'I told you last night that you're too valuable to me. I can put a lot of pressure on you, Rusty.'

'People you can pressure are valuable to you, are they?' I sneered. 'What about this Yanithos Collection? It's my guess that it's some set of jewellery that you want to steal. There's a burglar alarm system that you can't work out how to bypass and you want me to do it. Somewhere along the line there's another gang that doesn't like competition. That fits everything in.'

'Rusty, why don't you tell me what happened last night?' she said sharply.

I laughed.

'Hasn't he told you?' I asked. 'Doesn't he

dare come and confess failure to you?' She didn't answer that, so I gave her a quick summary of what had happened after I'd got home. When I'd finished I heard her breathing in short gasps.

'I don't know anything about that,' she said eventually. 'Even if I was working with Morgan's friends why should I bother to find out how much you know if you were going to be killed?'

'You'd want to be sure of what I've told the cops. For all you know Jackson could have shot his mouth off with the full details, for old time's sake, and I could have passed it all on to the police, to try and save myself.'

'Who do you think killed Morgan and Kathy?' she asked.

'I've no idea. Perhaps his pals had him killed. Perhaps he fell out with them or he wanted too big a cut of the loot for himself. Once he'd got me into it, I should imagine that he'd be pretty much a spare part.'

That made sense to me. The more I thought about it, the more sense it made. Suppose Jackson and his pals had had the idea of knocking off the Yanithos Collection, whatever it was. They couldn't bypass the alarm and Jackson saw me and told them that he knew someone who could.

Meanwhile, his pals start thinking that they can get along very well without Morgan Jackson. Perhaps it's some trouble that's been brewing for a long time. They have him killed, Kathy Newnes gets in the way somehow and has to be killed herself, and that just leaves me. All I need now are the names of Jackson's pals and it's over.

I explained this to her.

She listened in silence and then gave that well remembered laugh.

'You might be pretty good when it comes to playing the piano,' she said, 'but why don't you try and stop thinking about more complicated things?'

'Huh?'

'That may make sense to you but to me there are so many holes in it that it can't be true. If they need you to bypass this alarm, as you say, then why have you killed? Wouldn't that be like cutting their own throats?'

She had a point. To me, the way I'd reasoned it out had been so obvious that I'd missed the big flaw. I couldn't see any way out of it, but at that moment the doorbell rang.

'Look,' I said, not wanting to admit to her that I was lost again, 'there's someone at the door and I'll have to ring off. I might call round to see you again some time.'

'Make it soon,' she said in an amused voice. 'I can hardly wait.'

I dropped the receiver onto its prongs and went to the door. The bell rang again before I got there.

'All right,' I said impatiently. 'I'm coming.'

I was very wary about opening it. I slid the bolt back and turned the knob, keeping hold of it and standing so that I could throw my whole weight on the door and slam it shut if necessary.

I peered round the edge of it.

'Good morning, Mr Barlow,' Superintendent Vanning said, 'Worried about something?'

III

It was on the tip of my tongue to tell him I hadn't been worried about a thing until now, but I changed my mind. In my experience, policemen don't like cracks like that; it makes them even more suspicious than they are normally. Instead I gave what I hoped was a welcoming smile and opened the door wide enough to let him in.

Sergeant Corfield was with him. They

trooped in and gave keen glances round the flat, making me glad that I'd moved that poker as soon as I'd got up, and then sat down on the settee.

'What can I do for you?' I asked, sitting on the arm of one of the chairs and trying to look casual.

Vanning leaned back as if he intended to stop for the day.

'We'll only take up a few minutes of your time, Mr Barlow,' he said. 'There's something that we'd like to check with you.'

I waited.

He slid his hand into his inside pocket, took out a wallet and flipped it open. I took the white bit of card that he handed me. It was an official looking, postcard sized picture of the man who'd attacked me last night. After staring at it, trying to keep the alarm off my face, I looked back at Vanning.

'What's this?'

'Have you ever seen him before, Mr Barlow?' he asked, watching me.

Afraid that if I spoke my voice gave me away I shook my head. At the same time I looked down at the picture again, so that he couldn't see the expression on my face.

'Are you sure?' he insisted.

'I'm certain. It isn't the sort of face you

126

forget. Who is he, anyway? Is there any reason why I should have seen him?'

Corfield cleared his throat.

'Just to take an example, Mr Barlow, you don't remember him coming into Meecham's, do you?'

'Not that I know of but that doesn't mean he hasn't been there. I'm there to play the piano, you know, not to look around and see who's come.'

'We appreciate that,' Vanning said, 'but we just thought you might have seen him. You're not playing the piano all the time. Or are you?'

'No, I alternate with a disc jockey. Why don't you ask him if he's been there? All he does is play records and weigh up the birds, and he could have seen this character at some time.' I was starting to get irritated by his attitude. 'Who is he anyway?'

'His name is Mickey Waite,' Vanning told me. 'Did Morgan Jackson ever mention him to you?'

'Let's get this straight,' I said. 'I knew Jackson up to about two years ago. The only time I saw him after that was for twenty minutes in the bar at Meecham's. He didn't have time to mention very much to me.'

'And Mickey Waite was one of the things

he didn't talk about?'

I nodded.

'I've never heard his name until now,' I said truthfully. 'What's the trouble with him, anyway?'

'He's a tearaway,' Vanning said bluntly. 'Whatever racket you care to name, Waite has been involved in it. Usually he acts as a strongarm character. Someone else runs the rackets and anyone on the receiving end who gets uppish has Waite put onto him. We know that he's operated as minder manager at a few clubs and we thought you might have seen him at Meecham's.'

I shook my head.

'No one's running a protection racket at Meecham's,' I said, 'so there's no need for any gang to have a minder manager to collect their end of the take every week.'

'How can you be sure there's nothing like that going on?' Corfield put in.

I was starting to get a little hot under the collar. From the way these two were going on anyone would think they'd decided already that I'd killed Jackson and were just trying to prove it.

'I'm not sure,' I said. 'If you want to find out for certain why come to me? Why don't you ask Benny all about things like that. All

I know is what he tells me.'

'We've traced a connection between Waite and Morgan Jackson,' Vanning said. 'That's why we came to you, to see if you know anything about it.'

'Well I don't,' I said shortly. 'Getting any nearer to finding out who killed Jackson?'

'We've a few leads.'

'As long as I'm not one of them.'

He looked at me with interest.

'Why would you say that, Mr Barlow?'

The trouble with coppers is that they think everyone's got something to hide. A lot of us have, but it doesn't make it any easier to have a conversation about them.

'No reason,' I said hastily. 'I'm just trying to make a joke.'

He smiled thinly but if he thought it was a curious thing to make a joke of, he didn't comment. I handed the photograph back to him and he replaced it in his wallet.

'I don't want to sound awkward but ought you to have shown me just the one picture?' I asked. 'I thought that in cases like this you gave people a bunch of photos and hoped that they'd pick out the right one.'

'We do sometimes,' he agreed, 'but as it is Waite isn't a suspect, he's just a line of enquiry. What we'd have done if you'd said he had been at Meecham's or that you knew Jackson had been seeing a lot of him, we'd have made further enquiries and maybe pulled him in. If we'd done that we'd have lined him up with eleven other blokes picked at random and asked you to identify him.'

It didn't seem to make much difference to me. Either way the cops had him and once he was in their clutches they weren't likely to let him go. Even if they hadn't been able to pin either of the killings onto him they'd have got him for something else. Perhaps I should have said that he was here last night trying to beat my head in with a steel rod but that would have raised trouble for me. If he wanted to kill me there had to be a reason, and finding that reason meant enquiries could too easily come back to Fingal's.

They might still do that, whatever I did.

'What's your next move?' I asked Vanning.

'Keep plugging away at it,' he said. 'It's a lot of routine work now, that's all, until we get the answer. We've a couple of dozen coppers going round asking questions of various people who we think might be on the fringe of it. Something will break soon and then we'll collect the pieces.'

'You make it sound easy.'

'It wouldn't be for one man,' he said.

'There are so many of us that we can do a lot of things a man on his own could never do.'

That's where the police have their advantage, of course. There are so many of them that once they get their teeth into something it's very hard for it to get away. Of course, he could have been saying that as a warning to me, but that was something I didn't want to think about; besides, I didn't see how he could have known I was poking around.

Unless Steve Ashworth had told him. They'd have got round to seeing him now, because his name would be in Kathy's address book.

But if Ashworth had said anything, Vanning would have given me a much stronger warning than that. I got the impression that Ashworth was like me, and didn't want to have too much to do with the police.

On impulse I said: 'You might know the answer to this, Mr Vanning. Ever heard of the Yanithos Collection?'

'The what?' he snapped. He leaned forward to stare at me, and even Corfield seemed surprised.

'The Yanithos Collection,' I said, wishing that I'd never opened my mouth.

'It's a large collection of antiques and jewels, worth about sixty or seventy thousand

131

in the right markets,' Vanning said. 'About six months ago it was stolen. Why should you bring it up now, Mr Barlow?'

Chapter Four

I

We must have stayed motionless for at least half a minute, staring at each other, while I tried to think of some explanation other than the truth. Eventually Sergeant Corfield moved and cleared his throat. This seemed to break the spell and stop the spiral of thoughts that was forming in my mind, going round so that I couldn't break out of it and think of anything new.

Vanning leaned back again, a frosty smile on his face and the fingers of his left hand slowly bending and writhing, like a heap of snakes on the arm of the chair.

'Well, Mr Barlow?' he asked. 'It's a funny thing for you to bring up out of the blue like that.'

'I thought you might know,' I replied lightly. 'It was something that cropped up at the club last night.'

'In what way did it crop up?'

'You know how it is,' I said, smiling at him and hoping is wasn't as ghastly as my stiff lips told me it might be.

'I'm a policeman,' he said pointedly. 'I've never worked in a club. I've no idea how it is so you'd better tell me.'

'It was while I was playing the piano last night,' I said, 'The stage at Meecham's is low down and you can hear people talking if they're sitting at the front tables, or dancing near it. I heard two guys talking about this Yanithos Collection. One seemed as if he knew all about it and he was betting that the other one couldn't get him all the details by the end of the week.'

Vanning was frowning at me, as Corfield wrote swiftly in his notebook.

'It was some kind of boast that the second guy was making,' I went on desperately. 'That he could find out anything in a couple of days.'

'And what exactly did they say about the Yanithos Collection?'

'Nothing. That's the trouble. They got up and went to the bar halfway through, so I lost the rest of the conversation. It's been stuck in my mind ever since.'

'And you decided to ask me about it,' he said heavily. 'What did these men look like?'

'You sure know how to ask questions, don't you?' I said with another attempt at a smile. 'I can't help you there, I'm afraid.'

'Why not? If you heard what they were saying so clearly, then–'

'It's dark at Meechams,' I broke in. 'To me, they were just men. I could hear their voices but I was sitting with my back to them and I didn't want to stare at them, so I never saw them. It's like when you're sitting on a bus and the people behind you start talking. Besides, I was playing the piano.'

'Then how come you could take so much interest in the conversation?'

I shrugged.

'It gets boring up there sometimes. There are a few numbers which are always popular with the customers but you get so used to playing them that you don't have to think about it. They play themselves. This was one of them.'

'And the men walked away afterwards?'

'That's right.'

He pressed his lips together and glanced towards Corfield, while I sat sweating and trying to appear unconcerned. Actually, my own mind was buzzing with questions. If the

Yanithos Collection had already been nicked, why had Jackson been interested in it? Was he the thief and he wanted me for some sort of disposal job? That didn't make sense because I knew nothing about getting rid of hot antiques, and Jackson could have guessed that easily.

My talents lay in playing the piano and following burglar alarm circuits and I didn't see how either of those could be linked with a pile of stuff which had already been stolen. I'd been thinking ever since I woke up that I'd got everything pretty well taped, but what with this, and what Diane had said, I'd been knocked right back to first base and I hadn't a clue what I should do now.

More important than that was Vanning's reaction to the yarn I'd just spun him. Let him get the wrong idea and I wouldn't be doing anything except sitting round in a cell while he made further enquiries.

'I wish you could remember what these men looked like,' he said. 'It might help me a lot.'

'It isn't a question of remembering,' I told him, encouraged by the fact that he hadn't yelled for the handcuffs. 'It's a matter of not even knowing. They were behind me and I didn't turn round so I never even got a glimpse of them. I'm sorry, Mr Vanning.'

He shook his head slowly.

'That's the first break that we've had on that case since the stuff vanished. Are you sure that you can't tell me any more?'

He was practically pleading with me, which was a reaction I hadn't expected. I gave him the spiel again about how I'd be delighted to help the police if I could and eventually he gave up. Before he did, he tried the angle that even if I hadn't seen anything, someone else on the stand might have done.

'All the other guys are further back than I am,' I said swiftly. 'They can't hear anything because of the music and as there are sides to the stage they can only see straight ahead. They haven't a hope.'

'Then if you hear these men again, for God's sake turn round and have a look,' he said. 'I don't care what happens to the music. You'd be doing the police a big favour.'

Sure, I thought, as he stood up, I'm the man to do the police big favours. Here they are, working flat out to arrest me one minute and wanting big favours doing the next. I told him I'd give it a whirl if I heard anything, then showed the pair of them out.

I didn't breathe easily until the door

snapped shut after them and even then I wasn't fully relaxed. I poured myself a quick whisky and sat down to do some heavy thinking. I wasn't much better off at the end of it, and I decided that the only thing to do was go and see Diane again. Of all the people I'd met since seeing Jackson again she was the one most likely to know what was going on. I was going to get it out of her if I had to twist her arm. She wouldn't pull any more stories on me, that was for sure.

So that she wouldn't have any warning that I was coming, I didn't phone her. I went straight downstairs and got into my car. The traffic held me up a lot but I used the jams to work out what I was going to do and what I was going to say when I saw her. For a start I didn't believe this nonsense that she didn't know why Jackson had wanted me. She was his mistress and there was no reason why he couldn't have told her, especially if she worked with him in his other rackets.

The only thing I could think of was that he might be contemplating getting rid of her, but in that case why leave her in that luxury flat. Wouldn't it be simpler to just turn her out into the street?

And if she knew too many secrets, he could get rid of her permanently. Even if he didn't feel like killing her himself, in his line of business he'd have plenty of friends willing to do him an efficient cut-rate job. Possibly she'd seen the signs and bumped him off, before he could get round to it. My flesh crawled at the thought that by going to see her now I might show her that I knew too much. Next time she sent Mickey Waite he might not miss.

I wasn't as long getting there as I'd expected. I drove into the car park, switched off the engine and sat for a few minutes, going over what I wanted to know, the questions I was going to ask and so on, then I opened the door and started to get out.

As I did so, someone came out of the back entrance to the building and began to walk towards a car some distance away from my own. He had his back to me, but there was no mistaking that figure and that shambling, hunched way of walking.

It was Benny Sugar.

II

Someone used to this kind of work would have known exactly what to do. I hadn't a clue and I just stopped there, half in and half out of the car, while Benny shambled over to the far side of the car park, and squeezed between another row of cars. I lost sight of him then but a moment later a door slammed and there came the whirr of an engine starting.

I got back into my car as quickly as I could without drawing attention to myself and sat with my face turned away from him until I was sure that his car had passed.

There was no proof that he'd been to see Diane but to my way of thinking it was virtually certain, and if Benny was involved it introduced something new into things.

It meant that I hadn't been brought into it because Jackson had happened to see me on a chance trip to Meecham's. Benny could well have mentioned my name to Diane or Jackson at some time and the information had been stored away. So again, that meant Jackson wanted something which was uniquely mine. And as I couldn't see him having any use for my piano playing it must be that he was interested in burglar alarms. But the Yanithos Collection had already been stolen so that couldn't be what he was after. If it was something else I was lost, of course, but Kathy Newnes had mentioned the Yanithos Collection so there was a link somewhere. And whatever was involved it would have to be something big to make it worthwhile to kill Jackson and Kathy and attempt to kill me.

While I was sitting there hesitating, trying to fit in this new bit of information before I went to see Diane, another car came into the car park. I didn't take any notice of it at first then I saw something vaguely familiar about the man who was getting out of it.

Mickey Waite.

He slammed the car door and walked towards the flats, his lips pursed in a whistle. A few moments later he disappeared from sight and I decided to stay around for a few minutes. Much as I wanted to see Diane, I wasn't going to her flat while he was there, that was for certain. Besides, I could see Diane at any time but an opportunity to follow Waite might never arise again. Provided he wasn't too long I could spare the time to sit around until he came back, then go after him.

He wasn't as long as I'd expected. No more than five minutes, in fact. He was still whistling and it would have been hard to imagine anyone less like a murderous thug than the man who was crossing the car park. It was a warm day and he was dressed in a lightweight suit, snappily cut, with a narrow brimmed trilby on his head. He walked jauntily, as if he hadn't a care in the world, and unlocked the door of his car again.

I started up my own.

He reversed faster than I'd have cared to myself, drew forward and moved away. There was a little shriek of tyres as he accelerated out of the car park, and I went after him.

Following another car is hard at the best of times. I don't know if you've ever tried it, but I hadn't until then and I was unpleasantly surprised to find out how difficult it actually is. In the kind of traffic I was having to deal with there would have been quite enough to do watching for ordinary idiots, without having to keep an eye on a vehicle several cars in front as well.

We headed out of London. Fortunately he didn't seem in a hurry, in spite of the Grand Prix manner in which he'd left the car park and he was content to dawdle along in the same lane, only swopping when he needed to, for right turns and so on. I fell into a routine, and I was just getting used to it when he fooled me by suddenly swinging left without a signal, or even a flash of brake lights to show that he was slowing down. I heard horns hooting behind me as I slammed on my brakes, and turned into the side street just in time to see him turning off again.

Carefully, I followed him. He seemed to know where he was going, which was more than I did, and then I lost him. I didn't realize it for a couple of minutes, but after driving down a long street of terraced houses, littered with dogs and small children, it dawned on me that I hadn't seen him for a long time.

I reached the end of the street. He hadn't been down any of the streets turning off this one, and he wasn't here either.

He'd gone.

I stopped, then turned left and pulled into the kerb.

Something struck me then that should have been obvious as soon as he'd turned off the main road so abruptly. He'd known that I was following him and had twisted through the side streets just to confirm it, throwing me off as soon as he was sure.

I looked round nervously.

Now that he was sure of it I expected to see him sneaking up behind me, with either a gun or iron bar. Only a group of kids were on the pavement, though, and I relaxed again. Presently I started the engine, turned the car and drove back to the main road.

I could always have returned to Diane's, as

I'd intended, but there was now Benny Sugar's part to clear up. I remembered how he'd questioned me the other night about Morgan Jackson, probably fishing for the gang and seeing what he could turn up. Perhaps if I got hold of him and told him that I knew about his connection with them I might come across something interesting myself.

Diane was shrewd and hard. Even under pressure she was quite capable of thinking up some story which would cover the facts and fool me, but Benny, I suspected, would be different. He'd soon crack, I had no doubt, and if he didn't it would be easier to use force against him than against Diane.

Finally, if I went to Diane and asked her what he was doing there was nothing to stop her fobbing me off with some cooked up yarn and then calling him and telling him to put over the same story. If I went to see her, I couldn't ask her about Benny, which was what mainly interested me, without the chance that she would warn him. If I didn't ask her about him I would have to see him anyway, and soon.

So I went to see him. I'd always known that he'd lived quite high, and I'd reckoned that Meecham's must be raking in the shekels for him to be able to afford it. I'd envied him for being able to live like that, but now I wasn't so sure. If most of his money came as a spin-off from Jackson's rackets, then I'd rather have had my own place and my old heap of a car instead of Benny's, which is this year's model.

I stopped outside his place, went up the stairs and rang the bell. After a wait of a minute or two I rang again, and heard footsteps shambling up to the door. There was a sound of a bolt being drawn back, then it opened and I saw Benny's stomach, immediately followed by Benny himself.

'Hi, Benny,' I said, resisting the urge to poke him with my finger, just to start the softening up process.

He gaped at me as though he couldn't believe who I was. His eyes blinked, and he rubbed his face with the back of his hand. He hadn't yet shaved, from the rasping sound it made.

'Rusty,' he said at last. 'What brings you round here? It must be something urgent if it can't wait until you get to Meecham's tonight.'

'It is urgent,' I said. 'Can I come in?'

That seemed to bring him round with a start. He stepped back and opened the door wider, standing to one side so that I could squeeze past his enormous stomach.

'In there,' he said, waving his hand towards a half open door.

I went in and then stopped, just inside the room.

It was a swell room, though not quite up to Diane's standards, and nothing that I hadn't expected. The kind of carpet that gives you the impression you're wading through it instead of walking on it. Reproduction furniture that could have come from a demolition site but actually costs plenty more than I care to pay. A big television set. An illuminated cocktail cabinet. A tank of tropical fish at one end of the room, with the fish flicking around in brightly coloured streaks, while a tube at the bottom of the tank blew a constant stream of bubbles which rose to the surface and burst.

It wasn't any of this which made me stop.

It was the sight of Vicki sitting on the settee.

She looked as startled as I was. She was wearing a black skirt and a white blouse with a lacey ruffle down the front, and held at the cuffs with tiny gold clips. She looked beautiful and I wondered what a hick like me had been doing thinking he could get a prize like that.

She smiled when she saw me.

'I didn't expect you to turn up here,' she said.

'Nor me you.' I went further into the room and sat down on a chair which looked uncomfortable and which was uncomfortable. I shifted some of the cushions which had thoughtfully been left on it so that they padded some of the bits of wood which were trying to stick in me and watched Benny as he mixed a set of drinks.

'I don't like to criticise your choice of furniture,' I said to him, 'but didn't these Victorians have anything a mite more comfortable than this?'

'All genuine stuff, that,' he said, handing me my drink. 'It isn't like this modern junk, you know. These chairs will last for ever.'

'That's more than I will, sitting in them,' I said, wincing as another of the carved wooden knobs stuck into me, and moving a cushion to cover it

'It's going up in value all the time,' Benny pointed out. 'It's not just furniture, it's a little gold mine. That ought to appeal to you if nothing else does.'

'Maybe it does,' I said, sipping the drink.

'What brings you round?' he asked. 'First Vicki and then you. And I've only just come in myself.' He rubbed his hand over his face again. 'I thought I might grow a beard,' he said apologetically. 'It looks a bit of a mess at the moment.'

I decided to wait a while. Vicki's being here complicated things, and I hardly wanted to start knocking Benny about, trying to force information from him, with her sitting watching. Apart from that, I wanted to know what she was doing here when she was supposed to be having a few days away from Meecham's, to get over everything.

'Don't be sorry for your face,' I said with a grin. 'I was passing and I thought I'd call in. If I'd known Vicki was here I'd have come a sight faster, I can tell you.' I turned the grin on her, and she raised her eyebrows.

Benny said: 'Vicki's come here with some curious information, Rusty.'

'What's that?' I asked, wary. Curious information could only have some bearing on the murders.

She hesitated, looking down at the carpet.

'Go on, love, see what Rusty thinks,' Benny encouraged her.

'I think there have been a lot of odd characters hanging round the club recently,' she said. 'What do you think, Rusty? I know you're tied up playing that piano of yours and you don't get as much chance to look round as I do, but I don't think you miss much. You must have seen them.'

'What kind of odd characters?'

'Spivs and so on.'

'You get them in all the clubs,' Benny said. 'You can't avoid it if the club's any good.' It might have been imagination but I was sure I could see a slight filming of sweat on his forehead.

'But we never used to get them at Meecham's,' Vicki insisted. 'Not out and out spivs, anyway, and those are the ones I've seen. Superintendent Vanning showed me a picture of a man called Mickey Waite. He wanted to know if I'd seen him anywhere. I said that he'd been to Meecham's once or twice.'

'When did he ask you this?' I put in.

'This morning. He said that he might have something to do with–' She paused.

'With Kathy?' Benny said softly.

'That's right,' she answered nodding. 'Though I don't see how he can have done. She didn't have any friends like that and I'm sure she didn't know Waite.'

'You can never tell,' Benny said, and this time there was no doubt about that film of sweat.

'I thought you should know,' she insisted.

'He knows already,' I said quietly.

That brought both of them swinging round to face me. I used the moment to full advantage, taking a mouthful of whisky and letting Benny sweat some more while I swallowed it.

'What do you mean?' he said, frowning.

'Last night,' I said, 'you were asking me questions about Morgan Jackson. Right?'

'What of it? I was just interested. I wanted to know how well you knew him.'

'You said that you'd never heard of him and you didn't know anything about him. Today I find you're visiting the girl he used to go around with, Diane Thornton.' I gave him a hard look. 'What about that?'

'You're mad,' he said steadily. 'I've never heard of her. How could I visit her?'

'Benny, I saw you, not an hour ago. You came out of the block of flats where she lives and you drove off. You didn't see me.'

'Where does she live?'

When I told him he smiled and shook his head, while Vicki watched us as if she didn't know what to make of what was going on.

'That's where you've made your mistake,' he said, still smiling. 'I went to that block of flats because a friend of mine lives there. I didn't realize that anyone connected with this business lived there, too. If I'd known, I might have called on her.'

'What's this friend of yours called?'

'Martin Hughes,' he said after a moment. He didn't sound too convinced as he spoke, and I certainly wasn't.

'Let's look him up in the phone book,' I suggested.

'Why?'

'Because I don't believe that he exists,' I said bluntly. 'It would comfort me if I saw his name in the phone book, with an address in that building.'

Benny ran his tongue over his lips. His face was shining and he looked very warm and uncomfortable.'

'He isn't in the phone book, Rusty. There was a mistake and he was missed out.'

'Then we can get it through the operator,' I said driving him on. The more he lied to me the easier it would be to crack him later. 'Go on, Benny, put my mind at ease.'

'You're mad. There's no need for all this. I know his number and his address and if you don't believe that he exists, that's your problem.'

'Nuts,' I said. 'There's no such person and you know it. Let's have it, Benny. Why did you go and see Diane? Just where do you come into this business?'

There was a pause. Vicki moved uncomfortably on the settee and I didn't blame her. The argument had taken my mind off how bad it was sitting in these chairs, but she wasn't as involved in it as me. I smiled at her, but she didn't smile back, just looked from me to Benny and back again.

'Well?' I asked Benny. 'Made up your mind to tell me, yet?'

'You're mad,' he repeated. 'Completely mad. This friend of yours being killed and the police asking you questions has turned your mind.'

'One more chance, Benny.'

He shook his head.

I stood up and went over to him. He cringed back in the chair. Even his stomach seemed to rear up in horror, as if it was afraid of what might happen to it. I grabbed his collar and yanked him half out of his chair. His face turned a brighter shade of red and his hands pawed feebly at his neck. I held him like that for a few seconds and then let him drop.

It says much for the anonymous Victorian workman that the chair didn't even quiver as his weight dropped into it. Like Benny had said, this furniture was solidly made.

'Rusty!' Vicki cried. 'What are you doing?'

'Trying to sort out one or two things,' I said grimly. 'Benny knows a lot more than he wants to admit and I've got to persuade him to change his mind.'

Benny was rubbing his neck and sucking air noisily into his lungs. He worked his jaw, swallowed a few times and then started to say something about his fictitious friend.

'Benny,' I broke in, 'either you can tell me the truth now or I'll hit you until you do. It's your choice.'

'There's nothing to tell!' he said shrilly. 'I can't do any more than–'

His voice choked away as I yanked him up again. This time I poked him gently in one of his chins before I let him fall. He grunted, but I grabbed him again before he had time to recover and was just about to hit him properly when Vicki screamed.

'Rusty, stop it! You don't know what you're doing! You can't think–'

'I know just what I'm doing,' I said grimly. 'Keep out of this, Vicki. It isn't the kind of thing you should be mixed up in.'

'Neither should you!' she shouted. 'The police should sort it out. It's their job, not yours.'

Even if I'd wanted to there wasn't time to go into details of my quarrel with the police. I turned back to Benny and got hold of him as he tried to wriggle away, pulling him out of the chair again and hitting him harder this time, without letting him go. A trace of blood appeared on his lips and he licked it away.

'Well?' I demanded.

He shook his head.

'There's nothing, Rusty,' he said distinctly, his chins wobbling. 'I've never heard of this girl, Diane, and that's the truth.'

The only way to make him talk was to forget that Vicki was there. I let go of him and caught him on the jaw with my fist as he fell. He rolled sideways and one of the wooden arms of the chair prodded his side sharply. He grunted and his face turned whiter than Vicki's blouse.

He opened his mouth and I hit him again. More blood trickled down his chin.

Vicki grabbed my arm. I thrust backwards to shake her off and heard her stumble. When I looked round she was picking herself off the floor, her face expressionless.

'I'm sorry, Vicki,' I said at once. 'I didn't mean to hit you.'

'You didn't hit me,' she said tonelessly,

153

smoothing her skirt. 'You pushed me and I fell.'

A slight sound from the chair, a creaking of an old joint, warned me just in time. Without turning my head I ducked and Benny's fist whipped over my head, just catching the top of it. I straightened up, turning at the same time, and grabbed his arm, twisting it round so that he was bent towards the floor.

'I'll bet you haven't touched your toes in years, Benny, have you?' I said. 'You're going to now, or I'll snap this arm in two.'

He yelled as I gave another twist.

'Tell me Benny. What do you know about Diane Thornton?'

He started to tell me that he didn't know anything but a slight jerk of his arm brought him up short. He groaned, trying to lick some of the blood off his chin. I gave another gentle squeeze at his arm and he gasped.

'I'll tell you!' he cried. 'Let go my arm and I'll tell you.'

I let go his arm and he sank back into the chair. I half expected some trick but he was too far gone for that, his face the same colour as the spotlessly white handkerchief which he took from his pocket and used to dab at his lips and mop his brow. When he was through he tucked it away again and tried to smile at me.

'You're a hard man, Rusty,' he said, his voice whistling in his throat. 'A hard man.'

'Never mind what I am, Benny. Let's have it about you and Diane.'

His mouth opened and shut several times but no words came out. I reached out to grab him again and he suddenly realized how easy it was to talk.

'Waite's at the bottom of it,' he said wearily. 'Waite and Morgan Jackson. They're running a protection racket between them, or at least they were until Jackson was killed.'

That squared with what Vanning had said.

'Go on,' I told him. 'There's more to it than that and I want to hear the lot.'

'It started about six months ago,' he said after another pause. 'Waite came to the club one night and asked to see me. He told me that I'd better pay him what he wanted or I wouldn't have a club by the end of the month. I tried to resist, threatened to call the police and have him thrown out, but he just laughed and told me to think about it.'

He paused, then dabbed at his face with the handkerchief again.

'What happened?' I asked.

'Nothing. At least, not right away. I didn't

155

see Waite for over a week after that and I was just thinking that I'd done right to make a stand against him when it started. Someone broke in here while I was out. They smashed the television and three whisky bottles at the wall. The place stank like a distillery.'

There was a sob in his voice as he said that but whether it was because his flat had been wrecked or at the memory of all that whisky going to waste, I couldn't tell.

'There were other things,' he went on. 'My car was damaged. A lot of the club records were covered with ink and torn up. A car nearly knocked me down.'

'So you paid them?'

'So I paid them,' he confirmed. 'I've paid them every month since then. Waite came to collect the money but it didn't take much to work out that there was someone behind him. I reckoned that if I could work backwards and find out who was really running it, then going to the cops might do some good. As long as I could only give them his name, it was no use bothering.'

'I can see that. He'd disappear and someone else would come in his place. And in the meantime, you'd have had one of your ears cut off. So what did you do?'

'I asked around. I've got friends in the club

business and I asked everywhere I thought there might be some information. It was a slow business because I couldn't be too open about it for fear Waite might find out, but eventually I had enough to make sense. The name Morgan Jackson cropped up a lot but I'd no idea who he was or where to find him. I still didn't dare go to the cops because there was no proof he was behind Waite.'

Vicki cleared her throat. Benny looked at her then back at me.

'Go on, Benny,' I said in a hard voice. 'I don't want to hit you again but I'll have to if your memory gets too bad.'

'I'm sorry, Vicki,' he said.

I thought it was an odd remark and Vicki herself looked bewildered. Benny managed a thin smile.

'It was Vicki who put me on the trail,' he said, so softly that I could barely hear him.

'Speak up Benny. Don't be frightened. The only time you need be frightened is if you decide that you've said enough.'

'Something Vicki said made me think that Kathy might be involved with Waite and this man Jackson,' he said, the words bubbling out of him so fast that some of them didn't quite manage to get past his teeth. It made it hard to tell what he was saying but there was enough to get the general sense.

'Kathy?' Vicki demanded, her eyes narrowing.

'I'm sorry, Vicki,' he said. 'I wouldn't have said it while you were here but he made me. It's Rusty's fault.'

She turned to look at me. I'd seen her every day for about three months and I thought I knew her whole range of expression, but this one was something new. There was a chill and a coldness about it that made me think I'd be lucky if she ever spoke to me again, let alone stayed friendly.

Behind her the fish made bright patterns in the water as they flicked about the tank, and the stream of bubbles rose steadily.

'How did you think Kathy was involved?' I asked Benny, trying to lessen the impact of what he'd just said.

'I didn't know. Vicki said something about her and a man called Jackson. I tried to follow it up but a couple of days later Waite came to see me again. He said that his mates knew what I'd been doing and if I didn't pack it in they'd cut my ears off and make me eat them. I packed it in.'

'You packed it in,' I repeated softly. 'It's a good story Benny, but I didn't hear Diane's name featuring in it. How does she fit in?'

158

'I'm coming to that if you'll give me time,' he said hurriedly. 'When I heard that Jackson had been killed I went into it again, because I thought that with him being dead the racket might fall apart. I wanted to know if there was just him running it or if there was anyone else.'

'And was there?'

'I'd found out before that a friend of Kathy's, a girl called Carol Latham–'

'Just a minute,' I said. 'What do you know about Carol Latham? Who is she?'

'I don't know very much. She's a model, but not the same as Kathy. She was all fashion work but Carol does a lot of book jackets and glamour, that sort of thing. From what I've seen of her she'll be pretty big if she gets the breaks.'

'Where does she live?' I asked, thinking of the girl I'd seen when I had been to talk to Steve Ashworth in Soho.

'I don't know. I saw her yesterday–'

'Where?

'In the street.'

I frowned.

'Don't be funny, Benny.'

'It's the truth. I–'

I picked him up and hit him. Vicki was sitting on the settee sobbing. I looked

159

towards her and she pushed her hand into her mouth as if she was stuffing a scream.

'You'll find her address in a book in the bedroom,' Benny babbled. 'I rang her up and asked her if she knew anything about it. She said she didn't know very much but she mentioned this Diane Thornton. I thought I'd call round and see her, so I went today.'

'Wasn't that dangerous if Waite was hanging about?'

'I didn't have any reason to think he'd turn up there,' he said. 'It seemed as safe as anything else that I'd done.'

'You missed him by about three minutes, if that,' I said. 'He arrived just after you left.'

I wouldn't have thought that his face could have gone any paler, but it did when I said that. His mouth opened and closed but he didn't say anything.

'What did Diane tell you when you got there? Was it worth the risk?'

'She didn't tell me a thing, because she was out. At least, there was no answer when I rang the bell.' Judging from the look in his eyes he didn't expect me to believe that and he tensed himself against another blow.

'Easy, Benny,' I said. 'I don't know how long you were up there, but Waite had no luck either. He was only away a couple of minutes so it looks as if he didn't get any answer either. I believe you.'

'It's the truth, Rusty,' he said earnestly.

'And is that all you know?'

He nodded.

Ignoring the way that Vicki was looking at me, I went into the bedroom. Lying on top of a dark oak dressing table was a small notebook with a soft leather cover. I flipped it open and saw names and addresses carefully arranged in alphabetical order. Out of interest I checked everyone's, from Jackson to Steve Ashworth, but the only one listed was Carol Latham's; after jotting it down on the back of an old bill I found in my pocket I tossed the book onto the bed and went back into the lounge.

Benny and Vicki were sitting just as I'd left them. Neither of them spoke. Benny watched me warily but Vicki gave me the look she used on the drunks who sometimes tried to grab her while she was going through her dance routine.

I said: 'I've got Carol's address, Benny. We'll leave it like that, shall we?'

'What exactly are you after, Rusty?' he asked, his voice stronger now that there was no immediate threat that I'd hit him.

'I'm not sure,' I said. 'Waite tried to pulp

my head with an iron bar last night and I want to know who's behind it and why he did it.'

'So you come here and beat up Benny?' Vicki said.

'It was his idea,' I told her, not in a mood for mincing words, even with Vicki. 'He had the choice of telling me or not. And it wasn't my fault that your sister was mixed up in this racket. Someone's trying to mix me up in it and I've got to do the best I can to get out of it. That's all.'

'You won't tell them I said anything, will you?' Benny demanded.

I shook my head.

'While I'm at it,' I told him, 'you'd better get someone else off your list of young hopefuls. I'm going to want some time off until I've cleared this up.'

'You can't walk out now!' he cried. 'I've already got Vicki off, and–'

'Benny, I'll be back when this is all sorted out and I'm sure no one's going to kill me.'

A gleam came into his eyes and I could see that he was going to get some of his own back for the way I'd been hitting him.

'Rusty,' he said, 'if you walk out on me now you needn't bother coming back.'

'Don't worry,' I said. 'If that's the way you

162

feel I'll clear out. I'll be seeing you, Vicki.'

She turned away. I hesitated a moment then went to the door. As I opened it I heard her murmuring something to Benny. I couldn't hear what it was and I tried to kid myself that I didn't care. I clattered down the stairs and out into the street, filled with a feeling of helpless rage against the people who were trying to drag me into this, raking up the past and now bitching up whatever there might have been between Vicki and me.

I went back to the car and sat there for a long time with my eyes closed. Suddenly I seemed to see Dave Stewart again; he was grinning, but when I sneered at the vision and opened my eyes, it disappeared.

I wasn't sure what to do now but it seemed to me on thinking it over that nothing I did could make things any worse than they were. I was feeling hungry, so I went home, had something to eat then took out the bit of paper with Carol Latham's address on it. By leaning over in my chair I could just reach the phone book. She was listed in it and after a moment I went to the phone and dialled her number.

She answered after two rings.

'Hello,' I said. 'My name's Barlow. I came to see Steve Ashworth the other day and you were there with a guy called Simon, shooting a book jacket.'

'Well? she said in a bored kind of voice.

'I'm coming round to see you.'

She giggled.

'I'm not that kind of girl, Mr Barlow,' she said with more spirit in her voice. 'If that's what you're after I can give you a few phone numbers.'

'I'm after a word with you.'

'I'm sorry,' she said. 'There's someone else—'

'Look, Carol, if you don't talk to me you can have the choice of doing one of two things. You can either tell the police all about it or I'll get Mickey Waite to come and see you.'

I hung up on her gasp, gave it a few minutes in case she rang back, then tried Vicki's number. There was no answer and after a couple of minutes I gave up. Maybe she was still with Benny.

It took me a lot longer than I'd expected to get to Carol Latham's flat. For a start a tanker had broken down in the middle of a road junction and I squatted there along with a few dozen other motorists while it was taken away. Then I had trouble finding Werley Street where she lived, and had to ask a couple of tough looking punks swaggering along the pavement. It was that kind of district. Everyone looked at me as though they were wondering whether there might be a percentage in cutting my throat, or sizing up how much my car might fetch on the hot market.

I ignored them, parked it on a demolition site and walked the rest of the way. Anyone wanting to knock that heap off was welcome to it.

Carol lived in a crumbling Victorian house which had been painted with crumbling Victorian paint and converted into flats. I shuddered when I saw it. The whole house had the crumbling, unkempt look which such places usually have and the brightest thing about it was the green of the weeds which grew on the drive and in the garden. I went into the hall and stepped back to let another guy come out. He looked at me keenly then went down the steps and disappeared.

A board in the hall told me that Carol Latham lived in a first floor flat. I went up to it, along a narrow passage and was about to ring the bell when I saw that the door was slightly ajar. I frowned. There was just a faint crack of light showing down the side, as if it had been pulled shut in a hurry and hadn't quite caught. The slightest movement could lock it or open it, depending on which way it was moved.

I rang the bell. There was no answer, and while the silence crept back along the passage and settled itself uncomfortably around everything I opened the door.

There was a faint snap from the lock but it opened easily enough. The flat itself came as something of a shock after the luxury I'd seen at Diane's and Benny's, though even if things were scruffy they were at least clean. Propped on a table by the window was a single birthday card.

I went over to it and took a look.

From Simon.

He was the male model character who'd done the strangling act at Steve Ashworth's. I shrugged. It was Carol I wanted to see; her relations with Simon weren't the slightest interest to me.

It looked as though she'd run out when I told her that I was coming round. If it wasn't very helpful right now it was at least a sign that I might be moving in the right direction and that itself was encouraging. I took a look round the living room without finding anything of interest and then went into the bedroom.

I stopped right where I was, by the door, thinking that the scene at Ashworth's was being repeated, just for me. Carol was sitting in an upright wooden chair, facing the door and wearing the black bra and panties. There were just two differences from the earlier scene.

One was that she wasn't tied to the chair but simply lolling in it. The other was that this time, the strangling was for real.

III

I didn't want to report it to the police but I had no choice. Things were so stacked against me this time that I couldn't even risk making an anonymous phone call, like I'd done when I'd found Kathy Newnes. For a start, both Benny and Vicki knew that I was coming here. As if that wasn't enough, that bloke I'd met when I was coming in had taken a good look at me and would be able to give the cops a fair description when they got round to talking to him.

The only thing in my favour was that there was nothing which would obviously link this murder with the deaths of Jackson and

167

Kathy, but I wasn't going to rely on things like that. There was altogether too much chance of Vanning finding out that I'd been here, and if he did and I hadn't reported it to him I was likely to find myself with a real problem.

Even if I denied ever going into the flat and just said that I'd knocked and got no answer, it wouldn't help me much; Vanning would go so deeply into my affairs that something would be bound to come out. If he ever heard about Fingal's, I was likely to be stuck with all the murders.

After all, if he tried hard enough he'd find someone who'd seen me at Turpin Street when Kathy was killed, and he'd use the Fingal affair as a motive for my killing Morgan Jackson.

Bad all round.

Those thoughts had gone through my mind while I was calling him, and they went through it even more vividly when I was sitting in a small room at a nearby police station with Vanning in a chair opposite me and a sergeant, not Corfield this time, sitting with a note book at a side table.

It was a depressing room, painted in sombre shades of brown and grey, with three chairs in it and two tables. Two of the chairs were lumpy, iron hard armchairs, while the sergeant's was a fairly modern affair of grey tubular steel. I noticed that one of the rubber caps over the legs was missing and as he wrote the chair rocked from side to side, tapping faintly on the wooden floor each time.

I wasn't under arrest yet but there was no telling how long that state of affairs would last.

Vanning pulled a crumpled packet of cigarettes out of his jacket pocket and offered me one. When I didn't take it he tapped his own on the table top then laid it on the arm of his chair without lighting it.

'Did you know Carol Latham well?' he asked.

'Not too well. I've only seen her once before.'

'I see. She was just someone you met at Meecham's, was she? You happened to overhear her talking while you were playing the piano?'

'She was just someone I met,' I said shortly. There was something in his manner that made me wonder exactly what he had found out since he had last seen me, a kind of sneering coldness which certainly hadn't been there when he had come to the flat with that photo of Mickey Waite.

'And why bring me into it?' he asked. 'Why not simply call the police? Is there some reason why you asked specially for me?'

'She was a friend of Morgan Jackson's,' I said easily.

'And what made you call round to see her?'

'I wanted to know what she could tell me about Morgan. He might not have been a very good friend of mine but he has been murdered, after all, and I wanted to see if I could help. There's Kathy Newnes, too. I'm pretty friendly with her sister, you know.'

'That's the attraction, is it?' He smiled faintly. 'Don't get in too much trouble for a woman, Mr Barlow. They aren't worth it.'

I could tell him a thing or two about that but I didn't bother. I contented myself with returning his smile and waiting for his next move.

'Tell me everything that happened from the time you left your car and came to knock on the door,' he said. 'I know you've already given it to the Divisional man, but I'd like to hear it again, if you don't mind.'

I told him. I said that one of the people Morgan Jackson had mentioned when he had been talking to me was Carol Latham. I hadn't thought anything of it at the time but then I'd heard that she was a model and it struck me there might be a hook-up between her and Kathy, who was also in that line. I'd phoned her and asked if I could come round. Though she hadn't actually said so I'd got the impression that there was someone with her, but I'd gone round just the same. The door had been partly open and when I'd got no answer to my ring at the bell I'd walked in and found her dead.

He listened silently, then leaned back when I'd finished.

'Did she give you any idea who was with her, Mr Barlow?'

I shook my head.

'She didn't even make it clear that there was anyone. I'm only assuming that.'

And that was one of the troubles. All she'd told me was that there was someone else, and from the way the conversation had been going then it could as well have meant that she already had a boyfriend. If she had been on her own when I'd called her, then the only person who could have arranged her killing was Benny Sugar. He needn't have done it himself, but he could have phoned someone.

Like Mickey Waite.

Everything he'd told me could have been a tissue of lies, but it wasn't that which worried me so much as the fact that Vicki might be involved with him. I'd never considered it up to now, but with this new twist it became a very real possibility; one of the reasons I was keeping Benny in the clear with Vanning was so that I could check it out before he started chasing Vicki.

'If there was anyone, it must have been someone she was very friendly with for her to be sitting around with hardly anything on,' he said. 'Unless he was a client, so to speak.'

'She told me she wasn't that sort of girl.'

His eyebrows raced up his forehead so fast that I wouldn't have been surprised if they'd flirted into the air.

'You asked her?'

'She told me,' I said. 'She offered me the information, I don't know why. Maybe she didn't like me or something.'

'Any reason why she shouldn't like you?'

I shook my head and he returned to his original line of questioning.

'So whoever was there was a friend of hers.' He pressed his lips together. 'You haven't seen her address book, have you, Mr Barlow?'

'Should I have done?'

'We can't find one,' he explained. 'Most model girls keep one because they rely on having a lot of contacts. If they can't get hold of people quickly or they can't be found themselves, they lose work. Kathy Newnes had one which was very useful. I'd expected there to be one here, but there isn't.'

'Maybe she wasn't in it in all that big a way, yet,' I said. 'From the look of her flat, it doesn't seem as though she was. Or maybe the killer took it because his name was in it.'

'Which implies that he's someone we might not trace without the book,' he said thoughtfully. 'That's always assuming that there is a book.'

It was starting to get too complicated for me. I'd already had a hard day, and even if I'd been going to the club I wouldn't have been able to get there in time now. It was probably just as well that I'd had the row with Benny; he wouldn't be in too much trouble because people are lining up to take your place in that sort of job.

'I can't quite see where you fit into this, Mr Barlow,' Vanning said. 'You were a friend of Morgan Jackson, fair enough, but on your own admission you hadn't seen him for a couple of years. The other person who's been killed, Kathy Newnes, had a sister who works with you. The links are there, but don't you think you're taking too much interest in what's going on?'

'What do you mean?' I tried to speak lightly but my face felt stiff and the words sounded muffled and clumsy, though Vanning didn't appear to notice anything.

'Let's start at the beginning,' he said. 'The first we heard of Kathy Newnes' murder was by a phone call from someone who didn't leave his name or say what his interest was. Know anything about that, Mr Barlow?'

'Why should I?'

'What were you doing that night?'

'I was at home. I have Tuesday night off and I was watching the television. I read a book, too. Nothing exciting and nothing I can prove.'

He let that go.

'The other thing,' he said, 'was that when I was at your flat you suddenly brought up the Yanithos Collection. Nothing's been heard of it since it was stolen six months ago. Why raise it now?'

'I've told you—'

'You told me a story about some invisible men at Meecham's,' he said dreamily. 'It sounded an odd sort of thing to happen, as far as I was concerned.'

'Well it was the truth,' I said, trying not to get too angry. 'Who stole it in the first place?

You don't think that was me, do you?'

He glanced to where the sergeant was writing all this down and then spoke in a mild voice.

'If we knew who'd stolen it, we'd have it back by now. I'm not making any accusations. For all I know, it could have been anyone, including you.'

'You've no clues?'

He hesitated.

'Not a thing,' he said finally. 'I think it's safe to tell you that.'

'What mightn't it be safe to tell me?'

'Ignoring that and getting back to this case,' he said, 'I've been asking a few questions today and yesterday. One of the things which interested me was the connection between Kathy and Jackson. He was a friend of hers, we know that, but why should they both have been killed? And where did this man Jagger, who was supposed to have rented the flat where Kathy died, fit into it?'

Jagger. That was the false name which Jackson had used when he'd fixed up the flat. I'd forgotten all about it, but of course it would be something else which the police would have to unravel painfully.

'And where does he come in?' I asked. 'If

she was killed in his flat, then the sooner you find him, the better it's going to be. Maybe he pinched the Yanithos Collection.' I stopped abruptly, wondering if I'd been too reckless.

'We can't find him,' Vanning said 'He doesn't exist. I won't go into everything, but we've established that the flat was rented in a false name by Morgan Jackson. Now you can see things coming together, can't you?'

'You mean you think he met her at Turpin Street, killed her, then went home and was killed himself?'

He shrugged.

'That could be it, though the tests that have been carried out so far show that Jackson probably died first. We think that it's more likely they were working on something together, and someone from a rival gang killed them. He had an office where he was supposed to be an astrologer, you know, but I wouldn't be slandering the dead if I said that he was involved in a lot of rackets that had nothing to do with the stars.'

'And where does that get you?' I asked. I'd noticed that the sergeant was still writing in his book, and though I didn't know too much about how the police worked that suggested to me that there was a point to this discussion.

'In itself, it doesn't get us much further on, but there are some other things,' Vanning said.

'Such as?'

'One of them is that Morgan Jackson was shot. We found a gun tossed underneath the bed and tests showed that it was the murder weapon. There were no fingerprints on it but we have another thing we can do with guns. We can compare bullets and say whether or not they came from the same gun.'

'So?' I said impatiently. 'I know that.'

'We checked the bullets from this gun in the files to see if they fitted with any other unsolved shootings. They didn't, but when we sent photographs of the markings out to other police forces in the country for them to check, it was a much more interesting story.'

'Why?' I asked, knowing now how Benny had felt when I had been asking him questions.

'Because the Manchester police phoned me very quickly and said that about two years ago this same gun was used to kill a watchman who surprised a gang of fur thieves at a warehouse owned by a firm called Fingal's. The watchman's name was Stewart, Dave Stewart.'

My mouth was so dry that I could hardly

speak. I'd never expected anything like this, but on thinking back I could remember giving the gun to Jackson in the van afterwards and telling him to get rid of it. I'd thought no more about it, but the swine must have kept it, either because he was too damned careless to get rid of it, or because he had some idea that it might strengthen his hold over me.

'Well?' I asked as these thoughts raced through my brain.

'They were very interested in Manchester,' Vanning said, 'and gave me all the facts they had. Apparently Stewart wasn't really a watchman but he'd agreed to go in that weekend because there was a valuable consignment of furs. No one thought there was much danger, especially as there was a newly installed burglar alarm. In the event, it was very cleverly by-passed by someone who obviously knew all the facts.' He paused. 'You installed that alarm, Mr Barlow. Remember?'

'I remember it vaguely,' I said. 'I used to install a lot of alarms.'

Vanning nodded.

'You left the firm on the same weekend as the robbery,' he went on, watching me closely. 'There was a bit of a surprise about that at the firm, Strong's, as if you'd done it on the spur of the moment.'

'I hope you're not suggesting that I had a hand in this robbery?' I said, while the sergeant scribbled it all down into his little book.

'I'm just making an investigation into a crime,' Vanning said smoothly, too astute to accuse me of anything that he couldn't prove, 'and I've found a thread which joins it to another unsolved crime. There's another point about when you left Manchester, apparently.'

'What's that?' I asked, although I had a good idea.

'When you left Strong's you wrote to them and said that you were going to see your sister in Glasgow. Have you a sister in Glasgow, Mr Barlow?'

'I had. She's dead now.'

'What was her address?'

'I can't remember now. It's two years ago.'

'You led an eventful life two years ago,' Vanning said. 'That means she must have died just after you got to Glasgow.'

'So?'

'What did you do then?'

'I came to London,' I said, because there weren't many other answers I could give.

'You didn't think of going back to Manchester, where you had a job? Even though you had given up your flat there.'

'I wanted a change,' I said, taking care to keep my voice level and not show any signs of the panic I was feeling.

'And you never even collected your cards and a week's pay that was owing to you?'

'I had other things on my mind.'

'I'll bet you had.' He shrugged. 'All that was two years ago, as you say. I think you've already told me that it was two years since you saw Jackson?'

I nodded.

'So there are too many things for me to be able to ignore them,' he said. 'Any explanations, Mr Barlow?'

'I can't explain it,' I said evenly. 'It's just a chain of things. Don't you coppers have some fancy name for it?'

'Circumstantial evidence?' he said. 'I've thought about that, but this is a little too circumstantial for me to be happy about it.'

'I can't help that.'

'If it wasn't for the interest you're taking in this lot I might not be worrying too much,' he said. 'You must agree that if you add that in as well you get a fairly substantial equation.'

'I think I ought to have a lawyer here,' I said carefully.

He laughed and rolled the cigarette backwards and forwards on the arm of his chair.

'I'm not accusing you of anything, Mr Barlow. I'm merely keeping you up to date with what I've found out. That's all there is to it. I thought that if I was frank with you, something which could help me might click in your mind.'

A lot of things were clicking in my mind, but none of them were the sort of thing which would help him. He didn't ask many more questions after I'd brought up the matter of a lawyer and about ten minutes afterwards I was in the street again, walking back to my car.

Remembering the kind of district I was in, I was a bit surprised to find that it was still there, though when I got into it there was a certain unfamiliarity about the driving position which worried me. After a moment of sitting there trying to remember what was different, I realized what it was. Someone had pushed the seat back, but hadn't replaced it in quite the right place. I altered it, then drove away.

First the trouble with Benny and Vicki. Now the lousy coppers were searching my car. They knew about Fingal's too, and that really brought me out into a sweat.

If they started pressing the matter of my sister in Glasgow, I was really going to be in trouble. I'd never had a sister, in Glasgow or anywhere else, and even if I made up an address they could easily check it and prove that it was false. With that and the gun the heat was really on and I felt that a trap was closing round me.

Vanning had eased off with his questions after I'd mentioned a lawyer, which meant that he couldn't prove any of it yet and didn't want to go off too soon, but it left me in a swell position. Both Scotland Yard and the Manchester police would be trying to prove that I was guilty, and that left only me with any interest in finding the real killer of Kathy, Carol and Jackson. And even if I managed to do that without feeling the heavy hand on my shoulder, Manchester would be after me for an explanation of the Fingal business.

I was in a jam. Vanning had only let me go now because he wanted to give me rope; what I did with the rope was up to me, but I had the feeling that the outcome would be pretty much the same anyway.

Chapter Five

I

By the time I got home it was going up for half past seven. I wondered whether or not to give Benny Sugar a ring at the club and find out how he was making out, but I decided not to, and made some tea instead. I put in some heavy thinking, going over everything that had happened since I'd met Jackson on Monday night, but I didn't get anywhere. Eventually, I went to bed, to be woken up at eight-thirty the following morning by the shrilling of the phone bell. If there's one thing which annoys me it's being woken up by the phone. I pulled the covers over my head to dull the noise as much as I could, and eventually it ceased. Just as I was dropping off to sleep it started up again. This time it went on and on and in the end I realized that the only thing to do was answer it. I got out of bed, padded into the living room and grabbed the receiver.

'Well?' I said in a hard voice, hoping to

frighten the caller into making it as snappy as he could.

It was Diane Thornton.

'You're up early, aren't you?' I demanded.

'That's right. I want a word with you, Rusty.'

'Go ahead. Don't let my manner frighten you.'

'I'd like to see you. It isn't something I can do over the phone.'

'Look,' I said, 'Right now I'm suffering from over-exposure to coppers and all I want to do is go back to sleep and get over it. What do you want. Is it urgent?'

She hesitated. The static on the line crackled faintly and then Diane spoke again.

'Is it true that Carol Latham has been killed?' she asked.

'What do you know about her?' I said sharply.

'She was another of the girls that Jackson used,' she said. 'There's a small piece in this morning's paper and I recognized the name.'

I told her what had happened. When I had finished there was a sound of heavy breathing on the line, then she said:

'Rusty, please can you come round?'

'And when I get there I suppose Waite will be ready for me?'

'Waite's been,' she said. 'That's what I want to talk to you about. I'm afraid of what he might do next.'

'I thought he was a pal of yours,' I sneered. 'What's happened to break up the happy home?'

'You were wrong. I told you that when you said I'd sent him to kill you. I'd never met him until Morgan was killed.'

'So where does he come in now?'

'That's what I want to know. Morgan was planning something big and everyone is assuming that I know all about it. I don't know a thing, Rusty, and I'm getting scared.'

Soothing scared females is a speciality of mine. Had it been anyone but Diane I'd have been round there without hesitation; as it was I waited just a few seconds while I decided I'd nothing to lose even if it was a con, and then told her I'd be round as soon as I'd had breakfast.

After I'd eaten I went to the phone and dialled Steve Ashworth's number. A girl answered, presumably the receptionist who had been missing when I'd been round, and a few moments later I was talking to Ashworth.

'What are you after now?' he said. 'I've a lot of work this morning. I wish I had the

185

time to go around playing at detectives.'

'What makes you think that's what I'm doing?'

'I've read the paper,' he said. 'You want to ask me some questions about Carol Latham, right?'

'As it happens I do. Have the police been to see you yet?'

'I haven't seen a copper, Barlow. They haven't asked me about Jackson or Kathy Newnes or Carol.'

'Did Carol have any boyfriends?'

'You're joking. You saw her, didn't you? Do you think she had boyfriends?'

'Was there any special one?'

'Not that I know of. Simon, that character you saw here, fancied her, but I don't think she was so keen on him. She told him it was her birthday yesterday and he sent her a card. She thought it was a big joke.'

'I'll bet she did.' That explained the single birthday card in her flat. It was funny that Vanning hadn't asked me about that, but I didn't imagine he'd missed it; probably in the flush of asking me about Fingal's and the gun he'd forgotten about. 'There was no one else special?'

'Not that I know of,' he repeated. 'She didn't tell me everything, you know. I was only someone who could give her work. I wasn't a special friend of hers. Do the people who get you to play the piano for them tell you everything about their friends?'

'They tell me hardly anything,' I said drily, thinking of Benny Sugar.

I rang off and then left for Diane's. I'd been hoping that Ashworth might know something but if he didn't there was nothing I could do about it. So that I shouldn't be too prejudiced, I didn't do too much thinking on my way to Diane's though I did look out for any coppers who might be following me. There was none, which was a surprise, and it was just short of ten o'clock when I pulled up in the car park where I'd seen Waite and Benny yesterday.

Diane opened the door almost as soon as I rang and stood aside to let me in. I went wearily into the lounge, expecting to see Waite grinning at me, but there was no trap. I sat down and turned to face Diane.

The first thing I noticed was that there was a big bruise down one side of her face.

'Been having trouble?' I asked.

'That was Waite,' she replied, leaning her head forward and pushing her hair out of the way so that I could see another ugly bruise on her neck. 'He did that, too.'

187

'When was that? Yesterday?'

She fluffed her hair back into place and nodded.

'Like I said on the phone, he seemed to think that Morgan was up to something and that I knew all about it.'

'What time was this?'

'After tea. Why?'

'No reason, I just like to get things straight in my mind. What did you tell him?'

She went over to the cocktail cabinet and mixed a couple of drinks. Her hands were trembling and I heard the bottles clattering against the glasses, although she tried to conceal it by talking loudly.

'What could I tell him?' she asked. 'I don't know a thing other than what I've worked out.'

'You didn't mention me?

'No, and neither did he.' She came over to me, looking as beautiful as I'd remembered her, and wearing a black skirt and white jumper. 'You've got to get me out of this mess, Rusty.'

I laughed and took the drink which she offered me, knocking back a good half of it at one gulp. I set the glass down on the arm of the chair and looked up at her. But for her bruises she was lovely and in any other circumstances I might have fallen for her line. She'd bitten me once before, though, and she was going to have to work damned hard to do it again.

To get away from that seductive smile I looked across at the small glass statue. This morning it seemed to have a sneering grin on its face, as if it knew exactly what was going on.

'I've heard it all before, pal,' it seemed to say. 'There's no way out.'

'Don't you believe it,' I replied silently, and then turned back to Diane.

There was nothing sneering about her smile.

'I've got to get you out of this mess!' I said. 'What about myself?'

'I don't–' she began, and then stopped.

'Go on,' I said. 'Say it. You don't care about me.'

She didn't answer.

'That was always your trouble wasn't it?' I said. 'You never did care about anyone but yourself. It's coming back at you now, Diane, and you don't like it.'

'Well?' she said tensely. 'Are you going to help me or not?'

'Listen,' I said, 'I had the cops at me yesterday. They're within a few inches of finding out everything about Fingal's and Dave Stewart and what happened in the past. If they do, I'm going to have to tell them your part in it and how you worked on me to get me in the position where I'd have to do what Jackson wanted. They don't know about you yet, but they will if they arrest me.'

'You wouldn't–'

I ignored her interruption.

'The only way either of us can get out of it is for me to find out exactly what's going on and turn it over to Vanning so that he doesn't have to do any more digging for himself. After that, we can both slide away. Agreed?'

'How can they find out about Fingal's?' she asked warily.

'Jackson was shot with the gun I had when Dave Stewart was killed,' I said, not being able to bring myself to say out loud that I'd killed him. 'They've got comparisons of the bullets. It's all scientific and cast iron but they haven't enough proof yet to arrest me and make it stick. If they get it for either of those, they'll line me up for the other murders.'

'And you'd tell them about me?'

'If I thought I could save myself by doing it, I would. There are girls I'd like to protect, but I'm afraid that you aren't one of them.'

190

'And I suppose Vicki Newnes is?' she sneered.

I pressed my lips together. She couldn't have known it, but it was the worst thing she could have said, reminding me as it did of what had happened yesterday.

'Never mind Vicki,' I said, 'just concentrate on yourself. You shouldn't find that hard to do. One way and another you're in as big a mess as me.'

She knew it too. I could tell that from the way her shoulders sagged and some of the glitter went out of her eyes.

'What are we going to do?' she demanded, her voice hoarse with emotion.

'Sit down and don't get so worked up,' I said. 'We'll get nowhere if we start panicking.' I waited until she had sat on the settee. 'What did Waite want? Why did he have to make those bruises?'

'He wanted to know what Morgan had been planning.'

'And when you wouldn't tell him, he hit you?'

She nodded.

'And what was Jackson planning?'

She pressed her lips together. I could see that she was going to tell me again that she didn't know anything about Jackson's

191

business and I spoke again before she could say anything.

'Don't deny it,' I told her. 'If Jackson was keeping you in this flat he must have told you something. Besides, you said you worked with him on his rackets. You must know what he was doing.'

She hesitated again.

'What did you tell Waite when he beat you up?'

'The same as I've told you.'

'And he believed you?'

'Yes.'

'Then he's a bigger fool than I took him for,' I said. 'Or perhaps he doesn't know how you can lie.' I gave her a hard look. 'Listen, kid, if you don't spill the truth and fast, I'll beat you up worse than Waite ever would.'

When she didn't answer I got up and went over to her, grabbing her arm and pulling her to her feet. She struggled but she couldn't break my grip. I tightened it, squeezing her arm like a rotten banana, and she suddenly went limp.

'Going to tell me?' I demanded.

She nodded, and I let her sit down. She rubbed her arm for a second or two and then started, the words spilling out of her mouth as though they'd been in training since Jackson had been killed, just waiting for this moment.

'It was about the Yanithos Collection,' she said, 'Someone stole it and Jackson had plans to steal it from them. It was hidden somewhere until the heat went off and he was working out a plan to take it himself.'

'Who stole it?'

'I don't know.'

'If I were in your position I'd tell the truth. If we find out who stole it, then we'll know who killed Jackson. From there, the rest should be simple.'

'That is the truth,' she said desperately. 'Waite wouldn't believe me, either.'

'That's because what you told him was a pack of lies,' I said. 'He's obviously one of the other gang and the big question now is who's he working with?'

'He didn't tell me.' She managed to get a lash of sarcasm in her voice and I could see that being on the wrong end of the stuff she normally handed out was burning her up. If I kept at her for long enough, I was going to get something really worthwhile.

'Were you in yesterday afternoon?' I asked. She shook her head.

'Does the name Benny Sugar mean anything to you?'

'Should it?'

'That's what I want to know.'

'I've never heard of him,' she declared.

That seemed to drop me back where I'd started. I finished off the drink while I worked out what to do now. She offered me more but I didn't accept it because I wanted to keep my head clear.

'Let's go over everything,' I said. 'Morgan Jackson came to see me at Meecham's. He told me he had a job for me, and used the threat of Fingal's to get me to meet him at a house in Chelsea, where he'd rented a flat in a false name. When I got there I found a dead girl. She turned out to be Kathy Newnes, Vicki's sister, and through that the cops got on to me. Among other things, Jackson had offered Kathy a job, too, and her sister had heard her talking about the Yanithos Collection, which is a lot of antique stuff that was stolen about six months ago.'

'You haven't sat still, have you?' she said, a note of admiration in her voice.

'A lot of people are hitting at me from a lot of different angles,' I said. 'It isn't wise to sit still in those circumstances.'

'Have you found out anything else?'

I nodded.

'I went to see a character called Steve

Ashworth, who as you know was a friend of Jackson's. I didn't get anything from him but while I was there I met a girl called Carol Latham. Apparently she was involved in a protection racket with Kathy Newnes and Jackson. Know anything about that?'

'It was just one of Morgan's rackets,' she said softly.

'And Benny Sugar was just one of the people who got caught up in it,' I said. 'Or so he told me yesterday.'

'Did he tell you himself?'

'I had to knock him about a bit first.'

She said: 'Whenever Morgan added a club to his list he used to go there himself, to make sure that it was worth his while. Don't you think he'd have seen you a long time ago if he'd been to Meecham's?'

I stared at her for a minute.

'Are you trying to say that Benny was lying?'

'He could have been, to stop you from hitting him.'

'But if he wasn't caught up in the racket, how would he know about it?'

She shrugged.

'I can't answer that. But if Jackson had known for a few months that you were working there, do you think he'd have left you alone? I take it from the way you're talking that Benny Sugar has been paying out for a while?'

I nodded absently. Jackson wasn't the type of person who would have kept quiet if he'd seen me a few months or weeks ago. At the very least he'd have been after me for blackmail. I couldn't work it out, and eventually I gave up.

'All right.' I said, 'forget it for now. Let's see what else there is. Waite came to beat my head in the other night but I got rid of him. Soon after Benny had told me that Carol Latham was in the racket I went round to her. She'd been strangled, like Kathy Newnes.'

'Which suggests that the same person killed them both. Did anyone other than this Benny Sugar know that you were going round there?'

'Yes,' I said bitterly. 'Vicki Newnes. And there could have been someone with Carol when I phoned. If there was, it must have been the killer, who thought that I was getting too close to him and killed her so that she couldn't tell me anything.'

'Either that or Benny phoned someone else as soon as you'd gone. Even Vicki could have done it, but I don't expect you to see that.'

It was a thought which had been growing on me for some time, even though I tried to push it away. I reckoned it was pretty unlikely that she was involved, with her own sister having been killed, but her story that she had called to see Benny because she was worried about spivs hanging round Meecham's could have been false. If it wasn't, then it drew Benny into it, and could make nonsense of everything he'd said.

It could also–

'Christ!' I said.

'Thought of something?' she asked.

'I think I might know the answer to all this,' I said, 'Benny could have arranged for Carol Latham to be killed and he could have found out through Vicki that her sister knew too much, and killed her too. Maybe she was double crossing them or something. He also knew that I was involved and he could have fixed up for Waite to come round and sort me out.'

'And where does that get us?'

'It gets us to the job that Morgan Jackson wanted me to do for him,' I said, certain now that I was right. 'If the Yanithos Collection had been stolen and hidden in the cellars at Meecham's, who better than me to help Jackson get it out?'

II

'I don't get it,' she said after a short pause. 'Do you know how valuable those jewels and antiques are?'

'Sixty or seventy thousand, isn't it?' I replied absently, still working out the details. She nodded.

'And if you have something that valuable to hide, would you put it in the cellars of a night club? It seems too risky to me.'

'It might seem risky to you,' I said, 'but you haven't seen the cellars at Meecham's. The building used to be a block of offices and I think a security firm must have had the ground floor because the cellars are made on the lines of a bank vault. Not as strong, of course, but the same principles.'

'How about the alarm?'

'There is no alarm now,' I said. 'No one ever keeps anything that valuable down there.'

'So why would Morgan need you especially?'

'He wouldn't. By that I mean that if I hadn't been there he wouldn't have bothered to track me down to open it. Any of his normal men could have done the job easily, once they knew the layout.'

I could see understanding beginning to dawn in her eyes.

'If I'm there,' I went on, 'I know the layout and everything else, then it makes sense to use me.'

'I suppose it does,' she agreed. 'So where do we go from here?'

'I don't know about you, but I'm going to Meecham's.'

'And you expect me to stay here?'

'Why not?'

She shrugged.

'There's always a chance that Waite might come round again. I couldn't tell him anything before because I didn't know anything, but now he could easily force it out of me. If he starts hitting me again, I'm bound to tell him, aren't I?'

'That still doesn't add up to me,' I said, with a worried frown. 'If Waite is part of the original gang he should be able to realise why Jackson wanted me. There's something wrong, even now.'

'I don't know what he's doing,' she said sullenly. 'A man like him doesn't have to have a reason for anything he does.'

I looked at her a little curiously. I still

wasn't sure about her and I wasn't at all keen on taking her with me on what could turn out to be a very tricky journey.

'You could lock the door,' I said. 'He won't know you're in and–'

'And he'll break in,' she said bitterly. 'It'll be even worse then because he'll know that I've got something to hide. Is that what you want, Rusty? Do you want Waite to beat me up as a way of getting your own back for what happened before, in Manchester?'

That wasn't a question which wanted an answer and in any case I'd no intentions of getting involved in an argument with her. If I wanted her to come with me to Meecham's I was going to make the decision, not have it made for me by a lot of sob stuff.

To gain a break for myself I stood up and went over to the window. Not many people were about, and those that were scurried up and down the street, completely immersed in their own affairs, knowing nothing about me or Diane and caring less. The only thing that would make them care was when they read the details of the murder case in the papers, and even then they wouldn't bother much unless it was something sensational.

Like me being charged with four murders. Dave Stewart at Fingal's. Morgan Jackson.

Kathy Newnes, Carol Latham.

Whatever I did, I could never beat a charge like that, and the only thing was to stop it being made in the first place.

If I found the Yanithos Collection in the cellars at Meecham's as I hoped, it still wouldn't enable me to prove to Vanning that I'd had nothing to do with the murders, but it would be a step on the way. There might be other things there, too, which would give me an idea what to do next. Meecham's was definitely the place to go, but only if I had a reasonable chance of getting in and looking round without interference.

And if Waite called on Diane again, she was likely to blurt out the whole thing to him.

Not that I'd blame her, if he started beating her up. The way round it was either to take her with me or send her somewhere else, where Waite wouldn't find her. But that would mean leaving her on her own and as I still didn't entirely trust her there was no telling what she might get up to if I did that.

All in all, it seemed safer to take her to Meecham's.

I turned back to the room.

'Well?' she asked, smiling faintly.

'You'd better come with me,' I said. 'I'm not doing it because I don't want Waite to beat you up. I'm doing it so that you can't start anything tricky while you're on your own. I want you to do exactly what I tell you. That understood?'

'Of course,' she murmured. 'When are we going?'

I looked at my watch. It was five to eleven.

'Now,' I said. 'If we leave it any later we might run into someone there. People might be there in the afternoon to get a routine together, but no one goes in during the morning because it's too early for them.'

We left a few minutes later. Diane had changed into fawn slacks and a brown sweater. She wrinkled her nose when she saw my car and I laughed.

'Not quite what you're used to, I don't suppose,' I said, opening the door. 'It's what you'll have to put up with now that you haven't got Morgan Jackson and his rackets to provide the loot.'

She got in and banged the door so hard that she nearly pulled it into the car after her. She glared at me and I started the engine and moved off.

'Frightened that the cops might tie you up with some of those rackets?' I asked.

'Not really. There was never any proof that I was connected with them.'

'Just like the old days. There was no proof that you were involved in that Fingal business but you were. You set me up for it and that makes you an accessory.'

She gave a short laugh. Her hand came out to touch mine in the automatic gesture she had, then was withdrawn quickly.

'You'll never prove it,' she said, 'so don't go thinking that you can get smart. You're on the hook Rusty and that's where you're going to stay.'

'What do you mean?'

'Nothing special,' she said lightly. 'Just that I'll have to look after my own income when all this blows over.'

'And you're intending to blackmail me?' We were caught in a traffic jam and I turned to look at her. 'Good luck to you if that's what you have in mind. The amount of money I can give you wouldn't keep you in cigarettes, never mind pay for that flat and all that goes with it.'

'Morgan always used to tell me never to turn away money,' she replied. 'He said that everything was useful, and a lot of small amounts were just as good as one big one, and easier to get.'

'Meaning that you've got a bunch of other mugs on the hook?'

'Maybe.'

'You're playing a dangerous game,' I said, 'and in any event, it won't work with me. Morgan was the one who could prove that I was at Fingal's. I think if you tried anything like that you'd get too involved. In any case, Vanning's too near the truth for a racket like that to work as well as it should. I reckon you're on a loser there, Diane.'

'We'll see.'

'Perhaps. I was afraid of Morgan and what he might do but I'm not the slightest bit worried about you, kid. If you've any ideas in that line, forget it.'

We drove on in silence. I wondered whether to change my mind about taking her to Meecham's. I could always drive her out into the country and dump her miles from anywhere; by the time she got back into London it would be too late for her to do any damage. That was fine in theory, but something held me back; I didn't trust her an inch and in spite of what I'd just said to her I still looked on her much as I would a basket of snakes.

I was fortunate and found a parking spot close to Meecham's but not so near that anyone else going there would be likely to see and recognize my car. We walked quickly. Neither of us spoke until we got nearer the club and then Diane said:

'How do you intend to get in? Or is housebreaking one of your talents, as well as fixing burglar alarms?'

'No need for anything like that,' I said. 'I've got a key. All we do is walk in as if we owned the place.'

The street looked forlorn and deserted in the morning. No one was about and nothing moved except a ginger cat which was skulking round an alley further along. It watched us in the way cats will when they've nothing else to do, then blinked and turned away when it realized that we weren't going to do anything interesting.

I unlocked the door and we went inside. There was no need to put on the lights; we didn't really need them to see by and just in case there was anyone else hanging about I didn't want to warn them that we were here.

'What do we do now?' Diane asked softly, looking round the deserted clubroom. 'I never realized these places looked like this when they were empty.'

'We make sure we're on our own,' I said, keeping my own voice low. 'I might have to make some noise to get into the cellar if I can't find Benny's keys and I don't want someone calling the cops while I'm doing it.'

Actually, if I couldn't find the keys which Benny normally kept in his office we were in a bit of trouble because without them I didn't think there was the slightest chance of opening that door.

We crossed the room, our feet making no sound on the carpet which ran round the edge of the dance floor. On the stage the piano was closed and the drum kit was set up behind it, gleaming faintly in the dull light. Next to them was Mike's control panel, a couple of turntables and a pile of records.

I pushed open the door near the stage which leads to Benny's office and led the way down the passage, past the dressing rooms and a store room. Diane's eyes were flickering from side to side as if she was expecting Waite to jump out from some dark corner, but I wasn't worrying too much about her.

We reached Benny's office. The door was closed. Sometimes he locked it, but this time it opened easily when I turned the knob. If there was anyone else here, this was now the only place they were likely to be.

I was right. The lamp on Benny's desk was switched on and swivelled to face the door. It blinded me when I went in, but not so much that I couldn't see who was in the room.

Benny was sitting bolt upright on a chair

at one side, looking terrified.

Behind the desk was Steve Ashworth.

III

'Come right in,' Ashworth said. He was smoking a cigar, and the smoke bit sharply at my nostrils.

I hesitated. If I stepped back and slammed the door there might just be a chance to get out before he could hit me with a slug from the ugly looking gun he was holding. I tensed myself then decided against it and walked into the room with Diane behind me.

'Close the door,' Ashworth said.

She slammed it shut.

I stopped in front of the desk, standing so that the light wasn't so dazzling, and Ashworth rolled the cigar to the other side of his mouth.

'You took longer to get here than I'd expected.'

'I'm sorry,' I told him. 'I was held up in a jam. I'd have driven over the top of it if I'd known you were waiting for me.'

He chuckled.

'You're tied up in a jam now, Barlow,' he said, waving towards a chair which was near

Benny, who still had the terrified expression on his face. 'Sit down and don't try anything funny.'

I sat down. Benny cleared his throat and I glanced sideways at him. The fact that he was here fitted in with everything that I'd worked out about him, but the expression on his face didn't. There was Vicki, too. I wondered if she had any part in this, or whether she was safe.

Diane stood near the desk. Ashworth ignored her, and she was clenching and opening her hands nervously.

'Where's Mickey Waite?' I asked. 'Isn't he joining the happy gathering?'

'He'll be along,' Ashworth said.

'And what about Benny? Why's he looking as if he's swallowed a bee?'

'Benny's position is a trifle delicate,' Ashworth said, glancing at him but not taking the gun off me. 'He owns this place but I'm in control. He doesn't know what to do about it.'

'You mean you stole the Yanithos Collection?' I asked.

That didn't worry him at all. I'd expected him to show some surprise when I mentioned it but he acted as though it was the most natural thing in the world that I should know about it.

'What if I did? he said. 'How does that help you?'

'You never know.' I turned to Benny. 'What made you let him put it in the cellars here, Benny?'

He swallowed and looked hard at Ashworth as if he was mentally asking permission to speak. Ashworth nodded and Benny said:

'That was the protection racket, Rusty. You know how things are in the club world. There were one or two little irregularities here and–'

'What he means,' Ashworth broke in, 'is that he wasn't paying his taxes properly and that not all the drink he bought came through the proper channels. You know all these lorry loads of whisky and cigarettes which are hi-jacked? Some of the stuff comes to Meecham's. It cuts the overheads.'

'But it leaves him wide open to people like you,' I said. 'So the cellars of Meecham's are full of stolen booze and knocked off antiques. That it?'

'That's it,' Benny said. 'You can see why I had to make up all that stuff about Jackson yesterday, can't you? I'd have been in a worse position if you knew all about it.'

'So you weren't involved in any of Jackson's rackets?'

209

He shook his head.

'And what about Carol Latham?'

'A pity about Carol,' Ashworth said. 'She knew too much.'

'And that's why you killed her,' I said. 'You were the one who was with her when I phoned yesterday. As soon as you realized that I might force some information out of her you had to kill her?'

He nodded.

'Let's see if I've got the rest of it right,' I suggested. 'It'll help pass the time on.'

'Go ahead. Show us how clever you are.'

I said: 'You and Carol and Mickey Waite stole the Yanithos Collection. You were running a protection racket before that and you'd got a grip on Benny Sugar because he was fiddling his taxes and operating in stolen booze. You made him put the antiques in the cellars here until the heat had gone off them. Right?'

He nodded and threw the end of the cigar into the waste paper basket.

'Then Jackson comes into it,' I went on. 'Somehow he found out all this and worked up a plan to steal the antiques back off you. If it worked you couldn't object to anyone who matters, and he'd make himself a nice profit. He came to Meecham's to weigh up the situation, saw me, and realized that I'd be ideal to give him all the information and help him pull it off. I could get in and out of Meecham's. I knew the layout. I was just the man.'

'That's what puzzles me,' Ashworth broke in. 'Just what hold did Jackson have over you?'

That was the first time I realized properly that Diane had kept the Fingal story to herself, probably thinking that it would make a good blackmail touch to tide her over hard times ahead. Not that I was really worried about the reason. She had done it and that made things easier.

'Never mind what hold he had,' I told Ashworth. 'I'm concerned with what you've been doing. Somehow you found out what Jackson was planning and you killed him. It was safe, you thought. There was no connection between him and you and nothing that could link him with the Yanithos Collection.'

'You've left a lot of holes,' Ashworth said. 'Can't you fill them in? How do you think Jackson found out in the first place?'

I thought about that for a minute and added it to a couple of other things.

'Kathy Newnes was a model,' I slowly. 'She worked for you and I suppose that during

211

one of those sessions she overheard something. She worked with Jackson in some of his rackets and I suppose she passed it on to him.'

He shook his head.

'Not as smart as you thought you were,' he said, 'Is he, Diane?'

I looked at her and saw that she was grinning.

She said: 'Morgan was planning to kick me out. I'd got used to living in style and I didn't want to be thrown out, kicked back into the gutter, which is what it would have meant. I knew that he was planning to pinch this stuff off Steve and I sold the information for a promise of a big enough share in the proceeds to make me independent.'

I let this sink in.

'Then you deliberately brought me here?' I said. 'That story about Waite was so much moonshine?'

'I'd have used my gun if I had to,' she said. 'You made it easy for me, though.'

'And how about those bruises?'

'There was a little disagreement yesterday,' she said sullenly. 'We managed to turn it to our advantage afterwards.'

'Then that was why you called me the other night,' I said. 'You didn't want to know why Jackson had brought me into this, you wanted to know how much he'd told me, and whether it was something that he'd said which had taken me to see Ashworth that afternoon.'

She nodded.

'And,' I went on, 'the thing that Kathy Newnes overheard wasn't that the Yanithos Collection was hidden at Meecham's but that Diane was double-crossing Jackson.'

'That's why we had to kill her,' Ashworth said smoothly. 'She was trying to blackmail us, threatening to tell Jackson if we didn't pay up. She was too dangerous because she could have let something slip to him at any time. She'd already told her sister that Jackson wanted her for a special job, but that was simply to throw her off the scent about what she was really doing.'

Diane opened her bag, fumbled in it and took out a gun. Closing the bag with a snap she came over to me and jabbed the gun in my back while Ashworth grinned.

'You're getting to be a nuisance, Barlow,' he said. 'But for you there wouldn't be any danger to us.'

I thought that I had the whip hand.

'If you kill me,' I pointed out, 'the police will know that something's wrong. As it is, they suspect me.'

'And they'll go on suspecting you if you kill yourself,' Ashworth said with a smile. 'The weight of it got too much for you. A multiple killer. You decided to end it all.'

There wasn't a good answer to that, at least not one that I could think of off-hand. Fortunately I didn't have to because at that moment the door opened and Waite came in. Everyone turned at the sound. All our nerves were stretched so tightly that we'd have turned at the sound of a pin dropping off Benny's desk.

It was probably the only chance I'd have.

I jumped up, swung round and thrust Diane back into Waite, then moved sideways, expecting that Ashworth would shoot at the spot where I'd been. He did. The bullet whipped past about a foot from my face and smacked into the wall. I was on the floor by now, wriggling round behind the desk. The lamp was still shining but I was well out of its cone of light and I didn't think he could see me properly. Risking a quick glance round I saw that Diane and Waite had sorted themselves out. Waite pushed her roughly out of his way as she fell near me.

As she fell Ashworth fired at me. I rolled over but I needn't have bothered; he was too hasty and his aim wasn't all that accurate. His bullet drilled its way into Diane's head.

I started to wriggle the other way, going along the front of the desk to where she was sprawled with her gun near her right hand. Benny was nearest to it but he was too busy giving an impression of someone who's been turned to stone to do anything. Waite was jumping towards me. I reached the gun while he was in mid-leap and turned it on him, pulling the trigger.

That was Diane's last laugh, because the damned thing wasn't loaded.

The hammer came down on nothing but the threat deflected him. He twisted himself to one side and as he fell Benny came back to life. He must have realized that the only way out of the mess he was in was to help me and he grabbed Waite.

A lot of the pent up feelings of the past six months, when he had had those antiques at Meecham's and couldn't do a thing about them, went into the blow. I saw Waite's feet leave the ground and his head snap back, then I had troubles of my own.

Ashworth pushed the desk over and as lamp, papers and an inkstand showered down on me he jumped towards the door, pausing only to send a bullet smacking into the top of the desk, uncomfortably close to my head.

Scrambling up, I went after him. I wrenched open the door and went out crouching, so that if he fired he would most likely shoot over my head. At first I couldn't see him but then I made him out, running towards the stage.

I went after him. He disappeared into the main club room and when I got there I was in the middle of the floor before I realized he was up on the stage hiding in the shadows.

'Well?' he said, gasping for breath. 'Come on up and get me, Barlow.'

'You planned to double cross everyone, didn't you?' I replied. 'You gave Diane a gun to help her get me here but so she wouldn't be a danger to you when you decided to kill her you made sure it wasn't loaded. Were you planning to kill her?'

He chuckled. It was an odd, chilling sound coming out of the darkness of the stage, but it was better than a bullet.

'She wasn't going to get a share of the money, that was for sure,' he said. 'She was nothing without Jackson. She gave me the tip-off but she'd have to look out for herself after that.'

'I should have known you were involved,' I

said, 'There were no attacks on me until I'd been to see you, and then everything started happening.'

He chuckled again.

I'd been keeping him talking all this time, while I'd been backing slowly along the wall until I came to the doorway that we'd just ran through. My heart was thudding as I realized more and more that this was a last throw and if I failed I should probably be killed. My breath began to come in short gasps but I'd got it under control by the time I reached the door.

I couldn't see him now but I knew where he was. As I'd told Vanning, there are two side pieces to the stage which block the view of anyone at the back, where Ashworth was, so I knew that he couldn't have much idea of what was going on. Quickly, I went back into the passage, turned sharply and went through the door which leads to the back of the stage.

When I peered through a crack between two boards, I could see him standing absolutely still, peering into the gloomy room, his gun half raised. I suppose that with not knowing the layout of the place it must have seemed to him that I'd just disappeared, but he'd held all the advantages for too long.

I stepped through the door, on to the stage.

He must have heard some sound because he started to turn. He wasn't quite quick enough. As he brought the gun up we crashed down, with me on top, and before he could twist his arm round to get the gun pointing in the right direction again I was banging his head on the stage as hard as I could, my fingers twined in his hair. He lasted longer than I'd expected, twisting and writhing so savagely that he threatened to throw me off at any minute.

I smashed his head down with one hand. At the same time I drove my other fist into his face and he grunted sharply then went limp. Gasping for breath I staggered to the edge of the stage and jumped down. As I did so I must have caught the little box of tricks that Mike uses to control his coloured lights because when I looked back they were flashing on the unconscious form of Steve Ashworth, turning him red, then blue, then yellow, then starting over again.

Leaving him like that, I went back to the office. Benny was sitting on one of the chairs, holding his head in his hands, while Waite lay unconscious near the desk, where he'd been when Benny had hit him, and Diane lay at the other side.

'What a shambles, Rusty,' Benny said when I came in.

'Where's Vicki?' I asked him.

He looked dazed, as if he hadn't understood what I was getting at.

'Vicki,' I said 'Where is she?'

'At home,' He smiled faintly. 'There's nothing the matter with her, if that's what you mean.'

'That's what I mean,' I said looking round the smashed office. 'Why did you go to see Diane, Benny?'

He spread his hands.

'That part of what I told you was true, Rusty. All the arrangements for hiding that stuff had been done through Waite and I wanted to know who was at the back of it. I got nowhere until this started, and Diane's name cropped up. I thought she might be able to help me but she was out.'

'Probably lucky for you that she was. We'll have to call the cops, Benny.'

'I've already done it. They'll be here soon.'

As he said that we heard the faint sound of a siren, growing louder and louder. A few minutes later there was a hammering at the door and I went to open it.

IV

There isn't a great deal more. With both Diane and Jackson dead no one but me knew the full story of what had happened at Fingal's. It didn't take Vanning long to work out that they must have been involved in that affair together, and eventually he had to drop his suspicions against me and decide that I had nothing to do with it. Nothing he could prove, at any rate, which was just as good, though I didn't breathe easily until the trial was over.

I saw a lot of Vicki during that time, but I never made it up with her. That wasn't for lack of effort on my part, but even though her sister was shown to have had her fingers in a whole bunch of rackets, with Ashworth and Jackson, it didn't help matters. I was the one who'd first made her face up to it, and that finished things between us.

I didn't stay around for long after the trial. Meecham's was closed and shuttered and there didn't seem a great deal of point in remaining in London when I didn't have to. I had some savings and after a slight struggle to convince the authorities that I was a responsible person I got my emigration papers for Australia.

On the morning of my departure I tried Vicki's number several times but there was no answer and eventually I had to leave for the airport. I never saw her again and as I went up the steps to the plane I turned for a last look at England.

There was quite a crowd milling about on the tarmac, and suddenly I seemed to see Dave Stewart's face again. As I stared at him he smiled faintly and raised his arm. The last I saw of him, he was waving me goodbye.

The publishers hope that this book has given you enjoyable reading. Large Print Books are especially designed to be as easy to see and hold as possible. If you wish a complete list of our books please ask at your local library or write directly to:

Dales Large Print Books
Magna House, Long Preston,
Skipton, North Yorkshire.
BD23 4ND